Amethyst

Nadia Partyka

Time waits for no one, so don't wait for the right time.

Meet the Gifted Celestials:

Achille	Master of Pain.
Aira/Pearl	Master of Elements (Air).
Amelia	Master of hard work.
Aphrodite	Master of Love.
Asher	Master of Happiness.
Autumn	Master of Seasons (Autumn).
Blue	Master of Sadness.
Carlos	Master of Freedom.
Chambray	Master of Materials.
Flame/Ruby	Master of Elements (Fire).
Fortune	Master of Luck.
Frey	Master of Weather.
Gina	Master of Music. Queen of Celestia.
Horace	Master of Time.
Ivy	Master of Plants.
Kenechukwulael onzebediahyekac hukwunal	Master of Macrocosm

Kemi	Master of Care.
Liliha	Master of Anger.
Loba	Master of Communication.
Malko	Master of Surprise.
Mizan	Master of Balance.
Morana/Amethyst	Master of Death, Illness and Misfortune.
Morpheus	Master of Dreams. Helping Max and Amethyst.
Naida/Sapphire	Master of Elements (Water).
Oba	Master of Kings. Father of Gina.
Odysseus	Master of Hate and War.
Persephone	Master of Destruction.
Rachna	Master of Creation.
Ravi	Master of Art and Drama.
Rawya	Master of Story.
Riki	Master of Strength.
Salus	Master of Health.
Sora	Master of Sky.
Spring	Master of Seasons (Spring).
Summer	Master of Seasons (Summer).
Taqi	Master of Fear.

Terra/Emerald	Master of Elements (Earth).
Themba	Master of Trust.
Tuesday/Amber	Master of Day.
Uki	Master of Space. Helping Max and Amethyst.
Valda	Master of Beings. Helping Max and Amethyst.
Wantu	Master of Greed and Want.
Winter	Master of Seasons (Winter).
Xander	Master of Protection. Helping Max and Amethyst.
Zosia	Master of Wisdom. Helping Max and Amethyst.

The Xavil (Ja-vil) is a Celestial's power source. It is the only organ other than the brain that Celestials have.

Prologue: Celestia

Date: Unknown

It is well-known that Time is a precious thing. What most don't know is that he is a cruel being and is not to be messed with. Unless you want pain.

Uki knows this better than almost everyone.

"Max. Max..." Horace's hands glide over the golden strands that hang from the ceiling, glittering despite the room's black walls and dim lights. "Max is a smart little boy," He murmurs, allowing his long, spindly fingers to fall. "Don't worry, Uki," He says, turning to her, sending a shiver down her spine as if an everlasting cold was settling in. "I won't hurt him... badly." A near silent snicker escapes him as he turns back sharply to the place where golden watches tick rapidly. Tick. Tick. Tick. He focuses on one watch in particular: Maximus Manga's.

Uki clears her throat, her eyes darting around as if looking for an escape. *"Sir, he is just a kid. He didn't know what he was doing. He doesn't deserve any form of punishment. He's too young..."*

"Fifteen is not that young," He interrupts, and rattling comes from next door, where his wild beasts live. "And even if he didn't understand it, he did it anyway." He says it like it explained everything. The rattling slowly grows louder during the tension between them. "Why didn't you feed them?" He asks as he holds the watch carelessly tight, almost crushing it.

I was busy. I have my own job to do, you know." Uki immediately regrets her tone.

Horace raises his head by a fraction of an inch. "I do, but you have always found a moment to do it. You know you could have just asked for some help?" She shrugs. If she could, she would set his own 'pets' on him. He has always been so careful... he wouldn't — no, couldn't — change now that Max changed things a little. Right?

"I know what you are thinking," His snake-like voice wraps around her, threatening to crush her ribs. "Max won't make Horace change. Horace has always been a good boy," He mocks. "Think again. I don't care for anyone. Not even you." He lets his grip on her loosen. "Now get to work before you suffer the same fate as him."

"You wouldn't..."

"I would," He challenges her, but she backs away, knowing that going against him won't help. "Run along now."

"You do care for Morana, though." Uki sighs *"You've become so reckless since she left."* She backs away towards the doorway. "She would be destroyed if she saw you like this."

"Good thing she will never see me like this, then." When Uki is gone, Horace promptly calls up his model of Time and Dimensions. Lights of all colours dance across it, weaving in and out to make an intricate web. He sighs before slowing everything in the room down ten times. "Where are you hiding?" He mutters. After poking around a while, he finds what he is looking for: a minuscule lime-coloured dot near the centre of the model. "Peek-a-boo," Horace grins before gasping. If he had a heart, it would have jumped right out. A lilac dot. Right next to Max's "It can't be." Redetermined, Horace snarls, "I'll fix it all. I always do. I'll get Morana back. And I'll get rid of Max." He hates the word: Max.

Everything turns jet-black.

Chapter 1: Max

Welcome to my life, dear reader. Aren't you excited to read about the world's most pathetic punching bag? At least it takes you out of your own life and problems, then you realize my life is worse and you'll feel better. Wait. My life isn't worse? Is that a challenge? Keep reading, because I want to prove you wrong.

Date: Jan 8th, 2024

Thump thump thump. My feet slam the wood with enormous force each step. Thump thump thump. I was certain my alarm would wake me up this time. I slip and slide along the freshly cleaned floor, waving my arms in hopes of keeping my balance. Bang. I crash into the classroom door, seeing the plaque reading 'history' on it; at least it's the right room this time. Smack! I get knocked onto the floor as Ms. Williams opens the door. "Late, I see!" She yells, not even asking whether I'm ok after my fall.

Rubbing my aching forehead, I try to explain, "M-my alarm didn't g-go off!"

"I'm not going to take your excuses, Maximus. Now get up!" She huffs. I scramble for my glasses.

"C-can I g-go t-to t-the nurse, miss? I-I c-can't see properly. I-I think I hit my head really hard." I massage my head to exaggerate my point.

"No. You've already wasted enough of the class's time. In!"

"B-but I'm seeing double!" I attempt to enter the class through the wall, but only end up with my head throbbing worse than before.

"Stop complaining. Do you want detention? Hmm?" She flicks her hair and struts into the classroom.

"N-no miss." I grab my bag after a few swings of my arm and enter through the door, trying to use the power of echolocation.

"Max is blind everyone!" Alex shouts from his seat. "How will he read now?" He makes a fake pouty face in both my lines of sight.

"I-I'm not blind. I-I am seeing double."

"Quiet, Max! Have I not warned you enough?" Miss Williams snaps, and Alex makes a face at me behind her back.

"S-sorry miss." I make myself as small as possible and sit behind my desk, taking out my history book, pencil case, and notebook.

Miss scoffs loudly, not even trying to hide her distaste for me. "As I was saying... the Tudors were a famous royal family from 1458 to 1603. King Henry the Eighth was the first Tudor monarch, and he established the dynasty after winning the War of the Roses..." I frantically write notes while trying to remember everything. History is my favourite subject, and although I know a lot about it, there is never only one side to a story, or in this case, history.

Unfortunately for me, Shanon (my learning partner) decides to take a nap on my pencil case at some point, and I need another pen! I just ran out of ink and we're talking about all of Henry's wives, and I can never remember Catherine of Aragon. This is urgent! "S-shanon," I hiss. "C-can I have my pencil c-case? I-I need a pen." They don't even twitch at their name. "S-shanon?" I ask a little louder. I want to know everything.

"Maximus!" Please don't send me to her office. *Please don't send me to her office.*

"H-hey Miss?" My mouth acts faster than my brain, and I suddenly want to disappear right here and now.

"The disrespect this child has! How dare you..."

"I-I j-just needed my pencil case. S-shanon fell asleep on it."

"Where is my wedding dress?" They ask, discombobulated from their dream. All my fellow students burst into a fit of giggles at their remark.

"And he blames his peer!" She announces to the laughing class. "Tell me one reason I shouldn't send you to the Headteacher's office!" She bellows, silencing the room in an instant.

"I-I didn't do anything..." My voice goes quieter than a mouse's.

Her deep brown eyes meet my own, and her gaze alone makes me feel like she is reading my soul. "Mrs. Manga's office, Maximus," She spits in my face, slamming her fists on my desk. I gulp. Her tight smile plastered on her horrid pale face haunts me as I leave the classroom and head down to the staircase leading to the Headteacher's lair. Déjà vu overcomes me. Or maybe I am being overwhelmed remembering every other time I have had a similar experience.

"P-please let her be in a g-good mood," I silently pray to God. However, the thundering footsteps I hear when I knock on the door indicate otherwise and I can tell Mrs. Manga is clearly not feeling generous today. I take a step back to avoid repeating the same mistake I made 30 minutes ago.

"I'm not a monster!" Mrs. Manga yells with bulging eyes. "Come on in already! I don't have all day, Max!" I shuffle into the room silently. "Well, spit it out!"

"I-It's nothing, Mum. I just..."

"Don't even bother saying another word! Whenever you say, 'it's just,' I can be sure that nothing but *lies* will come out of your mouth."

"T-then, c-can I g-go?"

"You're not going to excuse yourself when you have been sent to the headmistress's office! You will explain yourself right this instance!"

"I-I was late," I start.

"Well, no surprise there. You probably entered class like a clown," She remarks. She's not wrong: hitting yourself against solid objects multiple times must be hilarious for fifteen-and-sixteen-year-olds.

"I-It's a long story."

"Well, talking about it is not making it any shorter!"

"I-I g-got hit by t-the door," I give up.

"Don't you mean you hit the door?" Mrs. Manga exclaims, pulling at her hair in frustration. "You're getting detention, mister. Don't be late."

"A-at what t-time will my detention be?" I submit to the punishment because arguing will make it worse.

"Three o'clock. I just told you," She replies, marching behind her desk and getting to work with some papers. "No, you can't go. You will wait until the bell."

I take a seat on a plush red chair, relief washing over me that the conversation is over. However, when I leave the office to head to the toilets, my day takes a turn for the worst.

Ring. Ring. Ring. The bell rings.

I sprint down three flights of stairs, tripping a few times, to get to the toilets: my place of sanctuary. "S-sorry Shanon!" I bump into her, but I don't stop to apologise properly.

"Um" I leave them speechless. I slow down only to prevent more crashes as I finally reach the underground cubicles. Yes, our cubicles are underground. I sit on the toilet lid and supress my tears from falling down my face.

Why am I so unlucky? What did I do? It can't be... that. Nothing happened then. Nothing at all. I take a sharp yet refreshing breath. *This is no reason to cry, Max.* I tell myself sharply. *There are people who can't get food, and are tortured and you're crying over a bad day?* Get yourself together. I take out my latest read out from my bag and will myself to leave reality and enter fiction. But before I can even get past one page, a horrible sight meets my eyes.

"Hey Maxy!" Alex. I look down at myself. I didn't sit on the toilet lid... but in the toilet. My heart pounds. Click. He took a photo. I pull myself out and try and grab the phone from this hand. How could I forget to lock the door? And how could I sit in the toilet without even realising?

"G-give t-that here, Alex!"

"I-I'm s-so s-scared." He mocks. "Why would I give you my phone? It's my property." I think of my own phone, empty apart from my mum, dad and my sisters. But Alex. Alex will have about fifty friends there, if not more.

"P-please. I-I have never done anything to you." I can't imagine the scene. Wait. Never mind. I can, and I don't want to.

"I can do anything I want to you." He stuffs his phone into his pocket as he gets close to my face. "Do you want to know why?" I have to get out of here. "Because. You. Are. Weak."

"I-I'm not weak." He scowls and punches me in the face. I topple over and stay plastered to the ground as the muscle around my eye starts to pulse.

"Someone strong would fight me back." He turns his back on me and walks away, but he isn't far away when he sticks his middle finger in the air.

Ring. Ring. Ring. The bell rings.

I take my bag from the cubicle and charge to the nurse. No one is going to stop me. Knock. Knock. Knock. "You know the rule." The nurse tells me through the door. "No visits to the nurse during class." She sounds like a child reciting a line in a play.

"P-please, miss. I-I have been punched."

"Max? Come on in, dear. Tell me it's you next time." Miss Nightingale takes quite good care of me, compared to all the other members of my life. She coincidentally is also my grandma from my dad's side. "Now. Who was the awful creature who gave you that? Don't tell me it was that Alex boy." I nod tentatively. "My, my! Would you like me to talk to your mother? I am sure she would do something about all this."

"Y-you c-can try." *But I doubt it will work.* I finish in my head.

"Hurry off to lessons now, dear." Grandma tells me after patching me up a little. "I am going to talk to that mother of yours. Ta ta, dear."

"B-bye, g-grandma." She kisses my swollen eye and I head off to design and technology. I'm sorry, that is not what I meant to say. I was meant to say hell on earth. Couldn't she have kept me with her a while instead of taking thirty seconds to give me a plaster and a kiss?

⧗

"Max. Where have you been and what have you done to yourself, you stupid boy?" Asks Mr Zak as I enter engineering class.

"I-I was with the nurse." I look towards Alex, who sits next to my empty seat, "I-I got punched." I try and fail to keep eye contact with Alex, and he grins.

"Yeah, sure. Now sit down. Quickly." My steps are as slow as I can possibly make them. Maybe I'll get kicked out and I won't have to sit with Alex. "As I was saying, we are going to be in test conditions. All boys, apart from Max, please go get some spare desks. As always, no talking, no notes, only your pens on your desk." All the boys other than me head out to get tables. Yes! A test! No sitting with Alex! I dance in my head. "And then we will do peer assessing." Not a whole ninety minutes with him then, probably only twenty. Good enough.

Chapter 2: Max

Date: Jan 9th, 2024

My usual lonely table for one is taken by Charlotte and I wander around like a lost child. All the tables are taken. I'm going to have to talk to someone and ask them to sit down. It'll be fine. Right? Ha! A table with no one by it! Ah, but there is stuff on the table. Alex seems to notice the same as he whispers something that is sure to be horrible to his friends. He goes and occupies the table, despite already having his own. Who would be dumb enough to leave their stuff out, where Alex can reach it? He takes a seat and knocks the lunch box off the table, two sandwiches and a piece of chocolate rolling out. He places his feet upon another chair and smirks. I guess I will go and find somewhere to eat now.

"Hey, dude." A voice I recognise distantly calls from nearby. "Didn't your mama teach ya how to behave like a good little boy?" I spin around to find a tall girl with bright violet eyes and motorcyclist jacket striding past me and towards Alex. Phones pop up everywhere to record this momentous occasion. A girl is sizing up to Alex?

Alex seems unruffled by her booming confidence and cracks his neck. "And who are you?"

She flips her half-purple half-black braids back with a hearty laugh, "I am Amethyst. Nice to make your acquaintance." She holds out her hand.

"Oh, yes. Wonderful." He lowers his feet and steps towards her, but he barely reaches her nose. He shoos her hand away like it is pesky fly.

"Make room, will ya. I wanna eat my lunch, without having to worry about how badly I hurt ya." She lifts her head as she says it, and smiles. Cheers and yells come from the growing crowd, trapping me in between the two of them. The tension between them makes me shiver and cower.

"Someone is feeling brave." He replies, still unafraid. If I were Alex, I would get out of her way in a heartbeat. But maybe that's just me.

In one swift movement he delivers punches to Amethyst's jaw, side and stomach. Her hand stops him again and again as he tries to hurt her, but even when he manages to hit her, she seems to not feel the pain. She moves elegantly as if she was dancing ballet, not fighting. I've read about fights before, but I've never seen one like this before.

"Tusk, tusk." She grins. "Are ya not able to see that ya can't hit me?" He huffs and finally backs down.

"Go eat your precious lunch, then." He spits and walks away, shooing away the boos of the crowd as it disperses in his wake. Many guys go talk to Amethyst, but she ignores them and goes eat her lunch, as if she had only waved to a friend, not showed off her karate skills.

Girls come to laugh at her or gawk at her as much as I probably am, but she doesn't pay attention to them. Then, most of the boys in my year other than Alex's cronies, come to her to flex their 'muscles' and try to flirt with her. Her look of disgust as they blow her kisses almost makes me laugh.

Snap out of it, Max. You need to go find somewhere to eat. You only have twenty minutes now. I scavenge around for a table, having forgotten that they are all full.

"Hey!" Amethyst calls to someone behind me, and I look back. "Do ya want to come eat with me; ya look kinda lost." Ironic, since she's the new girl.

Eyes nearby swivel in my direction, and I'm momentarily stunned. Glancing around again, I realize I'm the only one standing. "M-me?" My mind malfunctions. It's a rare occasion to be included; especially by the cool girls who usually overlook me as if I'm not there. Or a piece of dirt.

"Who else? Mr. Invisible in the corner?" She chuckles and the words jolt me.

"Umm, I-I would like t-to sit with you. I-I g-guess," I manage to stammer. She flashes a wide grin at me as I settle down across from her. Even seated, her tall figure is clear, yet not in a menacing way. I turn my head to the left slightly, in order to hide my black eye.

Extending her hand, she unnecessarily introduces herself. "Hi. I'm Amethyst, I'm new here. What is your name?" Hey eyes match her name, and I wonder whether they're coloured contacts. I take a few quick looks at her eyes, which speaks volumes and tells me that she will get herself in trouble any day.

"M-m-max," I stumble over my words more than usual as I briefly take her hand and jump back after touching her, like she is made of pure fire.

"Nice to meet you, Mmmax," She teases. What did I expect? I turn to my dinner tray and mechanically eat the now-cold lasagna and garlic bread. "Sorry. I'm new to this stuff." We eat in awkward silence, or at least I do. Amethyst seems lost in a tune. "This school seems really nice," She remarks, but I just shrug. "Could you show me where the science block is?" I nod. Does she genuinely want to talk with me? Or does she need a tour guide? Or does she want to somehow insult me? Or is this small talk?

"Huh?" Amethyst is somehow already halfway across the canteen, and I'm sitting with cheese dripping out of my mouth. "A-amethyst! W-wait!" I drop my tray onto the trolley and run after her, tripping over a few benches and chairs.

"Yes?" She turns to me politely

"T-that's not t-the way t-to t-the Science block." I pant. She cocks her head to the side. "I-It's t-that way." I point in the opposite direction.

"Thanks." She barely walks two steps before asking "Ya coming?"

"S-s-sure." I lead the way nervously. What to say? What to say? What would I want to be asked if I was new to the school? "W-where you c-come from last?" Damm it. "I-I mean, what school last you were? I-I mean... ugh." I push the heel of my palms into my eyes.

Amethyst chuckles. "You're funny, aren't ya?"

"I-I no know. D-don't know."

"Did ya mean, 'What school did ya go to before?'"

"Uh-hu." I nod. I don't trust words anymore: they always seem to fail me. We turn a corner and Amethyst walks so quickly; I have to half-run to stay in front.

"I don't know. My foster mum says I was St. Gizelle's, but I don't remember anything. I don't remember my primary school either." And she doesn't seem at all bothered about it?!

"D-did you g-go c-check whether you have amnesia?" I pull a non-existent bag strap over my shoulder and realise I left my back pack in the lunch hall.

She smirks. "I haven't truly considered that as an option, so no. And why at we at the canteen again?" I open my mouth to speak but...

Ring. Ring. Ring. The bell rings.

"I-I'm g-going t-to g-get my bag. I-I'll see you in c-class. B-bye." I rush off, leaving Amethyst to find her own way to science.

Chapter 3: Max

Date: Jan 10th, 2024

"S-so I g-guess I'll see you at my house later." I have a girl's phone number! I can't believe it.

"Yeah. Can't wait till our study session, I could really use some help with Newton's 3rd Law." She admits, rubbing her neck.

"O-ok. Um. B-bye." I head in the opposite direction than the crowd, clutching my book tightly. Kids eager to leave school push and shove against me as I weave in and out of them. Eventually, I reach the door I use. I use it because it leads to a great short-cut home and it's mum's private exit so it's never busy.

I run down the street from the school bus stop, take a left, a three-quarter turn round the corner shop and then a right to arrive at my humble home.

Where on Earth will Amethyst sleep? I should have thought of this earlier. I enter the house as quietly as possible to not disturb my dad. *Maybe my room? No. Mum would kill me.* I slip off my shoes, bag and coat. *The living room? We don't even have a spare mattress!* I go upstairs to tidy my bedroom. Oof. Books are spilling off their shelves, clothes are strewn across the floor, my desk is more paper than anything else and my window is blocked by Lego creations, making the room dark. *Attic? Yeah, there are some beds up there, and it's the cleanest room in the whole house. I will just have to do some dusting, that's it. And I'll have to make sure Amethyst doesn't look in the closet. Perfect. Easy.*

The stairs creek eerily beneath me as I make my way up to the attic. I switch the lights on and examine the large, almost empty area. This'll do. I take the two boxes of Christmas decorations and place them in my room. I'll have to lock it and the closet before she arrives.

"What are you doing Maxman?" Gabriella stops me in the middle of the corridor.

"I-I'm j-just preparing for Amethyst's visit." I drop my bag of cleaning supplies, pulling my plastic gloves off with no elegance.

"You, of all people, are having a girl round? Ooh." She teases, staring me up and down.

"N-no, G-gabs. S-she's my new friend." I try to convince her and sneak past simultaneously.

"Uhu." She says, clicking her tongue. "Tell me how it goes." She gives me a piece strawberry gum (which look old and half-melted) from the pack in her blazer pocket, winking at me before sliding the rest into her breast pocket.

"W-what am I supposed t-to d-do with t-this?" I call after her, but she acts as if she can't hear me over the clicking of her high heels. She swings her headphones onto her ears and starts singing loudly. What am I supposed to do with this? I put the gum in the bin I was carrying, leaving it in the entrance to my room, and go back to cleaning the attic. I do a little dusting and vacuuming whilst trying to recall where mum keeps the bed sheets.

I finish preparing the beds the second the doorbell rings, and I half run, half trip down the two flights of stairs. I swing the door open to find the postman giggling like a girl, though his mouth isn't moving. He passes me the package and clicks a photo for confirmation of delivery as he turns to reveal Amethyst hiding behind him. "W-welcome." I say, my brain understanding the situation.

She sniggers. "Did ya seriously think that only the postman was there?"

"Y-yeah." I flush.

I lead the way into the attic and extend the table with Amethyst's help. "Got your books?" She asks.

I had to forget something! "Mhm. I-I'll j-just g-go g-get t-them." I pop back downstairs to collect all my equipment and lock my bedroom door. As I reappear, I gasp in horror. "T-the c-closet." I squeal unnaturally high.

"What's all this stuff?" Amethyst asks with curiosity.

"N-nothing." I drop everything and slam the closet door shut, barely avoiding trapping my fingers and all of Amethyst.

"There certainly is *something* in there." She holds up a piece of parchment from behind her back and I rip it out of her grip. I slam into the closet again, so she won't be able to get her hands on anything else.

I take a deep breath and try to speak with confidence, "I-I t-told you, it's nothing. C-can you not snoop around?"

She merely rolls her eyes. "It was literally open and practically telling me to look."

I slide down the smooth oak in fear and ask. "H-how much did you read?"

"Up until 'In this closet'." I thought she wouldn't find out like this. I thought I would have time to prepare for what I'll have to inevitably say. "Can ya explain this? Please?" I stay silent.

What can I say? Hey Amethyst, it turns out that my ancestors have been working on a time machine, and I managed to complete it. But when I tried to use it, I basically destroyed all of time by sending the first humans all over time. "A-and you're one of t-them."

"Excuse me?" She raises her eyebrows, and I grow hot.

"Um. S-so basically, my, like, ancestors have been working on a form of a t-time machine... and yeah. I-I messed up c-completely." I sound like I'm talking nonsense. Amethyst squats down to be level with me and puts a hand on my shoulder.

"What do ya mean ya messed up?" She is oddly quiet, unlike her usual loud, powerful voice.

"I... I-I managed t-to finish it. I-I." I slow my racing breathing. "T-tried t-to use it, but it wasn't working well enough."

"Did ya time travel?" I can't read her face.

"W-well, yes, but it t-took me t-to t-the incorrect t-time and sent everyone from t-then t-to different points in t-the future." If her expression was unreadable before, it definitely is now. "B-basically, I made t-the first humans g-get sent out of t-their t-time. I-If t-they don't return soon, humanity will end. T-time will be reset."

"Why don't ya use your time machine, and get them back to their time?" I would laugh if I were to look back at this moment; I'm not that stupid.

"T-the machine is broken, and I don't know how t-to identify t-the k-key material."

"So, you're working from scratch and a lot depends on ya finishing this." I nod and Amethyst reflects my action. We both jerk back to standing position as we hear footsteps coming up the stairs.

"Maximus! What is going on here?" Mum stomps into the room with the anger of a bull.

"M-me and Amethyst are having a study session. I-I was assigned t-to help her with science." She slams the door and comes up to interrogate me, giving me a look that says it all: 'Study session?

Without equipment? By the wardrobe?'. When she looks at Amethyst, she suddenly turns into a loving character I wish I lived with.

"Come, Amethyst, you sweet thing. You must be hungry. Come eat with us. Max, go set up the table." I scurry out of the attic like a dog because that's the obedient boy I am.

"I can help, Mrs. Manga." Amethyst offers as mum drags her downstairs.

"No, no, dear. You're our guest. You sit down and relax." Mum leads her to sit in *my* seat.

Despite being our guest, Amethyst helps me set the table, and thank goodness, since I almost dropped four plates and three cups because of my nerves from our conversation. On the other hand, her presence also makes the pressure rise higher and higher until I feel like I might explode.

"What did ya mean by 'You're one of them' earlier?" Amethyst asks the dreaded question when mum is out of earshot.

I feel my face and ears go red, "E-exactly t-that." She freezes midway through laying out plates, as if someone had pressed pause. "A-amethyst?" She doesn't respond. I tap her gently and she collapses on the floor and the plates shatter. I cringe and wait for someone to scold me, but no one comes. Is she...

dead? No. Why would she be? It must be something else.

I look outside to see that dad has frozen whilst mowing the lawn and a bird is hanging in midair above him. I realise everything is silent. "W-what in t-the world?" Why has everyone stopped, like time decided to spontaneously freeze?

Before I know what I'm doing, I'm running into the street recklessly. As I stand on the road, cars and streetlamps glitch like in some old video game. "T-this c-can't be g-good." I spin in circles, taking in the madness and getting slightly dizzy. I snap into focus; I need to hurry up. I don't have much time left, if any at all.

I return to the attic, which seems like it could disappear with a snap of my fingers. I almost pull my hair out because of my nerves. I have to save the papers, otherwise I will have no way to create the time machine and go to the past and return the first humans to their place/time. I'll be the last human on Earth! Or was I already doomed to loneliness?

I grab the notes, but they are fading as much as the rest of the world. I can barely see the diagrams behind the purple, green and black. I pull out the message from my ancestors, which I already know by heart.

'Dear child, we may be gone, but our mission lives on. These plans, they hold the key to the past, present and future. Take care of all the progress in this closet and keep going.' I'm not even sure if this was meant to be for me, but it's my job now. Which I have failed at. I curl up into a little ball and watch the world flicker through the window as I pray to God.

As quickly as it had started, the world resumes playing, and I let out a small sigh of relief.

Chapter 4: Amethyst

Date: Jan 10th, 2024

"Mum!" I knock on her door for the seventh time, "You're going to be late for work!" I storm in and jerk the curtains open, letting rays of sunlight fill the dusty room and she groans. "Wake up, sleepy head." I pull her old, quilted blanket off her torso.

"Give me one minute." She moans and turns away from the window, pulling the blanket back up to her chin. "I've already given ya twenty! Anyway, I'm going over to Max's later. I'll be sleeping over there for the night."

"Mhm." She mumbles.

I yank a pillow from beneath her head. "You're not gonna get any more money from me when I move out, so get ya body out of bed and start making a living. Unless ya wanna live on the streets." I smack the pillow against her head angrily several times before letting it drop to the floor. "And she's still asleep. Just two more years, and I can move out." I sigh and shake my head. I prepare breakfast for myself and leave some boiled eggs out for mum. I head to school early and enjoy the time away from my household responsibilities.

I wonder what my foster mum would tell me if she were my actual mother. I would probably be dead because she is not mother material in any way, shape, or form.

⧗

"Max?" I ask, bewildered. How did I get here? I stand up utterly confused. Where is Max? He was here two seconds ago. I brush myself off and pick up the bits of shattered plates. I rub the painful spot on my head, wondering how this happened. I can feel a bruise forming where I must have fallen, but when? And why don't I remember it? "Max? Where are ya?" I yell in no particular direction.

"I-I'm upstairs." Is this guy trying to play a prank on me? He can't be. He's not that kind of person. I march past equally baffled members of Max's family to confront him. Is he seriously in the attic? When did he get there?

"What in the name of all things sacred did you do?" I demand, throwing the door open.

"I-It wasn't me." He tries to hide behind his thick chocolatey curls.

"Who on Earth knocked me to the floor and blacked me out then?" I cross my arms as I have seen some teachers do. I'm fed up with Max and I've known him only two days.

"I-I didn't, well maybe I accidentally made you fall. B-but you didn't blackout" He tries to defend himself awkwardly with his arms.

"So you're telling me that the master of time got angwy and evewything stopped moving?" I remember our conversation from earlier and mock him. But mocking him doesn't help me and my bubbling anger as I get closer to grabbing his collar and throwing him across the floor. I attempt to meet his gaze, to give him the death stare, but he looks into the distance at something I can't see.

"Y-yes. W-well maybe not t-the master of t-time. B-but," He chokes on his words as if in shock "E-everything froze." He grabs onto my shoulders as if his life depends on it. "T-the papers almost disappeared. I-I was afraid." He's stupid and talking nonsense. How can he seriously think I would believe this silly little act?

"Afraid of what?" I grunt.

"I-I was afraid t-that I would be t-the last human left." How ridiculous. This is all a big show.

"So why would you not freeze then?" I ask sarcastically.

"I-I'm not sure. T-the only difference between me and everyone else is t-that I have t-travelled in t-time. T-that might be why."

I back away from him abruptly. "Ya were serious? Ya actually..." I look down at myself. "I don't believe you. I'm just... me. I can't be a..." I don't know what to call myself as I recall the last words, he said to me before I blacked out. He finally looks into my eyes, and I can see in his that he is telling the truth. Unless he's a well-practiced manipulator, which I doubt.

"T-that's why you c-can't remember anything before. Y-you were never meant t-to c-come here." His hands drop to his sides. "I-I'm sorry." I hope I'll wake up and be relieved that it was a dream. Simply a dream. But my eyes never open. I don't suddenly come crashing back into consciousness.

"I hate ya." I spit at him, the bubbling anger inside me spilling out. "How is it that you managed to ruin my life twice?" I dig my nails into my palms to stop myself from beating him up, because he can't do anything if he's injured. "Ya will return everything back to how it's meant to be." I stress the 'will'. "And ya will do it soon."

"W-what do you t-think I have been doing? W-why do you t-think I'm always late? W-why I'm always learning." I don't want him to explain that he's been trying. I want him to do it. I need him to do it. We all do. I don't know what I'm supposed to say to him, so I leave in silence.

My house, (as in, my foster mum's house) is old, run-down and probably more than fifty years old. From what I know, it's never been repaired, but I like it any way.

As I do the dishes, washing and mopping, I wonder how my foster mum was expecting to be able to manage me and herself when she never does anything. I often think about that.

I change into my only dress that I love dearly. I would like to wear it every day, but mum says it looks bad on me, that I'm not feminine and that 'boy's clothes' look better. I wish I could make my own choices.

Soon enough, after a long, confusing chain of thoughts, my mind drifts to today's events again.

I guess it's a relief that I wasn't abandoned by some selfish parents who decided I wasn't good enough. But it's also a horrible thought that my real parents may have been inhuman or worse, non-existent.

I don't know why I'm bothering with mopping the house, since I never should have seen it. I was never meant to meet mum, or wear this dress, or think these thoughts. I was most likely meant to have babies to start humanity.

But since making a baby takes two humans were there others? Are they in this time? Do they know who they are? Does Max know where they are?

Max. The.. troublemaking, stammering weakling. My fists clench on the mop as I think of him. This time three days ago, I thought it was funny and kind of cute, but now it's sign that he can't do anything right.

"He can't do anything right." I whisper aloud. He's not going to be able to fix his machine himself. How long has he even trying? Since I remember things, right? So, about four months. Four months of no progress. "Ugh." I'm going to have to help him, aren't I? He doesn't deserve help, but I seriously don't trust him with the fate of the world. I'll talk to him at school tomorrow, but I'll make it clear that I don't want to do it.

I point the mop at the bedroom door, as if Max were on the other side of it and I could swing it open and attack him. That would be fun.

I hear the door downstairs click open. "Afternoon, Amethyst, dear. You won't believe what hap-pened at work today." I go downstairs, avoiding the weak points on the stairs. I throw my jacket over my dress before I reach mum's line of sight.

"Let me guess." I say, as I turn the stove off and serve soup. "Ya got fired?"

"No," She clicks her tongue, "Amethyst, where did you learn to be so pessimistic? I got promoted." From ridiculous item scanner to pathetic shelf stocker? I don't voice this, but it's a close call.

"Who are you now, then?" I hear that my own voice is too unnaturally sweet, but mum doesn't notice as she is pushing away the soup.

"I am now a deliveroo driver." I almost spit out my mouthful because of how pompously she says it.

"Congratulations." I swallow a potatoe slice whole and choke.

"I was hoping we could go somewhere to eat to celebrate?" She gives me the puppy dog eyes.

"If it's DrSer's, then sure." *We don't have enough money to treat ourselves to anything else because of her work situation.* I try to tell her though a gaze.

"Ok." she pouts like a child, and I pour her soup back into the pot.

"Get ready." I tell her and she jumps up in excitement.

Chapter 5: Amethyst

Date: Jan 11th, 2024

I ask the girl in front of me whether I can stand with her. She doesn't put up a fight and I slip behind Max in the lunch queue. I tap him on the shoulder, and I plaster a fake smile onto my face. "Hey Max."

"H-hi." He doesn't look at me, so I let my teeth bare under my kindly expression. "S-so you're not mad at me?" How can he hope for that?

"I am mad at ya. Fuming, even." He turns his back on me completely trying to disguise it as deciding what to eat for lunch, though there really aren't many options. "But I have come to the conclusion that you need my help, so." I clench my fists. If he isn't lying, then I want to meet the others, and if all goes well, I'll never seen him again. "I will assist you." He turns abruptly and looks at me with a hopeful, oddly doglike, expression. "But this does not make us friends." I warn him, but his joy does not dim. "I'll see ya in the library at three o'clock sharp. Don't be late." He better not forget. 3:01 and I'll be gone. He nods excitedly, collects his lunch tray and leaves.

I eat my lunch in peace, apart from the restless voice in my head telling me that I should be more careful around Max. 'He's sensitive. You're being too harsh. Can you be nice?'

Would you be nice to the person who stole your life without you knowing? Be nice to the person who might destroy everything because he thought he was being smart?

The voice goes quiet temporarily which feels like a petty, momentary victory. 'He's only fifteen!' It adds, almost stubbornly.

So am I. Well, I'm sixteen, but same thing! Why am I arguing with my own mind?

I am too nice to Max. I have given him five extra minutes to get here, and still nothing. In those five minutes, I scavenge around for any book about time, space time, and science in general. He arrives in a frantic mess at 3:05:32, the second I am seriously considering not helping him if he's always going to be late.

"S-sorry I'm late."

"I don't want to hear it." I cut in abruptly. "Did ya bring anything useful?"

"Y-yes. I-I brought all t-the plans. I-I see you've also g-got some books." He peers at my collection.

"I've determined that they'll be pretty useless. Sit down already." I seem to steal the words 'can I sit down?' out of his mouth.

He spreads out the papers, covering the whole surface, leaving no room is left for the books. We put them under our chairs for safekeeping and get to work analysing all the words. Generally, our time is silent, making me glad that Max got the hint that I'm not here because I like him. After three hours, we have absorbed all he information our brains can hold, and it's already dark when I head home.

My brain hurts from all the reading about space time, gravity, and all that nonsense. My mind feels close to exploding into a thousand pieces, but I have to keep it together. This is only step one. On the plan we wrote on during the session, step one is studying, step two is improving the plans, step three is gathering materials and step four is actually assembling the thing. Sounds simple when you put it like that, but this is a time machine we're making: a device that has never even created before, apart from the fifteen-year-old who messed up when he did.

I don't want to do this. I have to do this. I can't not do this. The world unknowingly depends on me and Max. I've been responsible as long as I can remember (which isn't saying much, but still) and I won't stop handling the pressure simply because it has multiplied.

Pressure makes diamonds, right?

I hear a loud bang from somewhere nearby, making my head jolt upward. I tell myself that some people still think they can shoot fireworks a week and a half after new year's. But this doesn't sound like fireworks. *You're over-reacting, Amethyst. Especially since you've only had about four hours of rest since you were plunged into all this.* As soon as I think about it, my eyes are closing on their own, and my legs feel ready to use their final energy reserves to jump into bed. But first I have to do the house jobs and my homework. I check my watch. 6:25. An hour and a half for studying, then an hour of housework. That's if mum doesn't come home before then. Add thirty minutes to cook dinner and ten to get ready for bed, I get 8:40 as my earliest bedtime. That's good.

I enter the house and shrug my outdoor wear off. I head to the kitchen, where there are sirens and red and blue flashes creep into the room from outside. They make my head hurt from the constant blaring. Was that bang really just fireworks?

I roll out of bed after another short night to find that someone has messaged me. It's... the school? I open it up, sitting up straight. When did they get my number? And why are they messaging me at 6:30 am?

"'We are sorry to inform you,'" I read aloud, "'That school is closing for the day.' That's great!" We'll have more time, and I'll get more sleep. But that isn't the end of the message. "'As the headteacher's son is hurt, and her wish is to close the school down for today.' Best wishes, what's his name?" That headteacher's son is a dumb boy. He must have gotten into some sort of accident that caused that bang yesterday. What's the headteachers name again? Goodness, I should know. "Thanks, anyways. You have given me time, and that's what I need right now. Time."

I shimmy under my duvet again, letting the warmth of my bed pull me downwards. My blankets keep out the cold. And though the world will never stop turning and working, all I care about right now is the comfort of contentment.

Chapter 6: Max

Date: Jan 11th, 2024

The end of Humanity fills my mind. Time is trickling away and I'm not doing enough. I can hear my brain whirring and my feet hitting the gravel repetitively. It's pitch black and no cars are around, so I keep walking blindly. I wish Amethyst would think of me as more than a piece of garbage she must deal with. I wish she would...

Footsteps.

Beeps.

Lights.

Booms.

Crashes.

Heartbeats.
Darkness.

Chapter 7: Max

Date: Jan 21ˢᵗ, 2024

I open my eyes, but everything is dark. What time is it? It must be late. I search for my phone on my bedside table, but a hand grabs my arm and holds me. I scream. "Shh. Shh." Hushes a... kidnapper? "It'll be ok. Don't worry Max." How does she know my name?

"W-why are you whispering?" I copy her tone. Stupid question. Out of anything I could have said, I asked the question with the most obvious answer- obviously, a kidnapper doesn't want to be heard. It's so dark I can't see the silhouette of the woman still squeezing my wrist, but I'm afraid of her either way.

"You're screaming across the whole ward. You need to quieten down."

"W-what are you t-talking about?"

A second voice starts speaking to me. This one I recognise. "How bad is it?" It's so high-pitched, I know that it can't be anyone but Gemma.

"G-gemma? W-what's g-going on?" I hear a sniffle. Is she crying? "G-gemma?" She never cries.

"It'll be ok, buddy. It'll be ok." A sob. That's definitely Gemma, but what's she crying for? Why is she a part of this kidnapping?

"C-can you t-turn on t-the lights? I-I want t-to see you." Gemma is my favourite sister, and she's the closest to my age too. The last time I saw her crying was when our youngest sister died seven years ago. What has happened to make her cry this time?

"It's that bad?" She asks the other person, her sobs renewed and even worse than before.

"W-what's bad?" What is going on? Why can I not see the outlines of anyone or anything in my room?

"I-I'm s-so s-sorry." Gemma wails. She is not one to stutter.

"W-what did you do?"

"I should have been there with you. I should have walked you home." She falls into another fit of tears, though she has never walked me home before, and rightfully so. She never wanted and needed to. I'm practically her age.

"Gemma!" I can't tell whether she is surprised by my outburst, but I do feel the atmosphere stiffen. "T-tell me what's g-going on."

The other voice speaks. "Good afternoon, Maximus." Afternoon? Pitch black? Doesn't she mean evening? Or night? "My name is Doctor Mary. You have been a part of a car accident."

"W-what?" Now that I think about it, I can't remember going to bed. But that doesn't explain why it's dark.

"You have gone blind. We are not sure whether it'll be temporary or permanent. And..." She continues, but I zone out. How can she say all this in such a calm tone?

"I-I'm blind? N-no. H-how will I?" Fix my time machine? Do my GCSEs? Read? Find my way around? I take a deep, not-so-calming breathe. "W-here is my mum?"

"I'm right her, Max." Her voice is neither soft, tearful nor sharp, making me unable to identify what she is feeling. "It'll be ok."

"H-how c-can you say t-that?" I scrunch my eyes closed. I can't stand the sensation of my eyes being open yet unseeing. "I-I'm blind mum! I-It's not ok. I-It will not be ok. I-I'm stuck like t-this." I won't cry. This isn't the end of the world. But it may bring the end... There are much worse things in the world. Hunger, poverty, the end of humanity. I start crying gently, but my sobs get louder and louder with each hopeless breath.

How will I fix it now? Does it matter? It was hopeless from the beginning. I'm only fifteen, and I can barely say out of the way of a car, so how am I supposed to do anything if I can't do that?

The events from (what I presume is) yesterday play backwards, from the moment the car hit to waking up in the morning, as if a tape was rewinding. The car hitting me. Me walking home from the library. Amethyst. Lunch. Amethyst. DT... "Amethyst!" I yell, forgetting where I am.

"Shush." The doctor tells me. "Do you need anything?"

"Y-yes. I-I need t-to t-talk t-to my c-classmate. A-amethyst."

"Is she the one you were out with that night?" Mum asks.

What's the right answer? The truth? A lie? "Y-yes." I am a terrible at lying. Mum would see right through me and suspect that I'm hiding something sinister.

"You will not see her then. She is the one who is responsible for you being here. She has given me more to pay for." What? She tuts in disapproval as if Amethyst took my sight, and not the car.

"I-It's not her fault." I stutter. "H-how c-can you blame it on her?" She does not reply. I demand to see her, but mum says no. I ask repeatedly, until she says she has to go work. "G-gemma? W-will you t-tell her at school? T-that I want I mean, need to see her." She doesn't reply. "Y-you'll be able t-to t-tell who she is. S-she's-"

"I know who she is." She says sadly and takes my hand, and my blood freezes. "You should stay away from her. She's a bad luck charm." My heart and soul ache to see. Gemma, Amethyst or even mum. Anything.

"W-what makes you say that?" I tilt my head, considering why she might be a bad luck charm. I thought the title was reserved for me.

"I'll tell you the story another day. It was over two weeks ago, so don't worry about it too much."

"T-two weeks?" She joined the school at the beginning of the term. How is that even possible? "H-how long have I-"

"You have been asleep about ten days." Ten days?! My breath starts to become more rapid. "Anyway, I'm going to go to school now, ok? I'll be back this evening or tomorrow morning." She has to leave right now? I have so many questions. I hear her get out of her chair.

"S-see you, Gemma. O-or maybe hear you. I-I mean, bye." I sit up in my bed slightly, though my head spins.

"Bye bye, buddy." She taps my leg gently and at the door the doctor talks to her.

The doctor speaks in hushed voice, as if she didn't want to be overheard. "It'll be ok, dear. You'll be taking him home tomorrow. Today we'll do a bit of braille and he'll practice navigating on his own. I'll make sure he'll have some fun." I pretend that I didn't eavesdrop. Everything feels so oddly real. When I went to the library that day, I couldn't have imagined this would have happened.

"D-doctor. C-can I please see Amethyst. I-It's important." I ask when she comes back over to me.

"Sorry. But I have no way of contacting her, and your mother and sister said no." A sudden breeze blows over my body as the doctor pulls the blankets off me. "Get up, now. You're going to have a lot of work to do if you don't want to be dependent on someone for the rest of your life." I roll out of the bed. *I am going to do this. Not only for the world I have put in danger, but also for myself.* "Good. Now follow me. Oops, I meant," I find an arm across my chest. "I'll guide you to the physical therapy centre: you haven't had any physical activity in over a week, and you need to do some exercise."

I am on the treadmill for half an hour, making me ridiculously tired: the doctor was right about me needing to exercise. I was never sporty, but now it's ten times worse. During my workout, I feel awkward and uncomfortable, as if going blind didn't only make me lose my sight, but also my purpose. It sounds ridiculous, but I'm shocked that I haven't randomly burst into tears. Not only do I feel mentally and physically weak, but I am trapped in my head with no escape. Only my hyperactive imagination and thoughts.

I am startled as the door slides open and Doctor Mary's voice stabs the near silence, her words sounding louder due to me having to rely solely on hearing.

"Whilst I was up at the ward, a lovely young woman claimed to want to talk to you." In a whisper, as if there was anyone else who could hear her, "She looks like an Amethyst." Doctor Mary has a habit of whispering unnecessarily. The door opens again.

My treadmill suddenly stops moving and I stumble into the machinery. "Would ya care to explain to me how ya blinded yourself?"

"Y-you don't know t-the story?"

"Of course I do. I want to know why you weren't being careful AND why you didn't care to contact me. I've been in the dark for over a week you

know!"

"I-I t-think t-that in t-this c-case, I'm t-the one in t-the dark."

"Ha ha. You're quite the comedian." I know Amethyst is crossing her arms across her chest and staring right into my unseeing eyes. Or maybe she has a pitiful look on her face, despite her sarcasm.

"I-It's g-good t-to know you're ok, t-too." I say aloud instead of my head, and I feel my face grow hot.

"Ya maybe," She exaggerates the 'ya', and the irony almost makes me laugh. "I am here trying to get into your house to get the dumb plans, only to find your mother attacking me with a broom, and..." She seems to remember that Doctor Mary is here, and though she wouldn't understand a thing,

Amethyst whispers, and I realise I'm starting to hate whispering. "And when I get to your stupid attic, there is nothing, and I figure out that everything is still in your bag." She broke into my house?

"H-have you seen my bag?"

"Me? I got here 20 minutes ago, and it's your bag. Ya should know where it is, not me."

"I-In my defence, I am blind. E-even if I looked for it, I wouldn't find it until it's t-too late."

"Great. Well, we've lost all of you ancestors' progress within two weeks of working on the thing." In my mind's eye, Doctor Mary is running her hands through brown hair, her sea-blue eyes wide in incomprehension. Unrealistic, since a doctor must always keep their cool, and I have no clue what she truly looks like.

"Do you... need your bag..." Asks the Doctor hesitantly.

"Y-yes. W-we have school project... stuff in it." Hardly convincing, but what was I meant to say? It's not a brilliant idea to tell her all about our top-secret plan for making a Time Machine.

"I believe that the driver of the car found it on the side of the road, then gave it to your father who I think left it by your bed in the ward." Doctor Mary informs us. Did Amethyst move? The air around me feels empty. I finally step off the treadmill, and surprisingly I don't walk into anything for a long while. But then I crash into the doctor. "Careful, Max. We don't want you in another coma." She chuckles and grabs my arms to steady me.

"T-thanks. C-can you t-take me," Then I quickly add "And Amethyst t-to t-the ward. W-we need t-the bag."

"You shouldn't be doing school projects right now. You should be resting.

"P-pretty please." I add.

Doctor Mary finally agrees and when Amethyst confirms that there is no one else in the room, she reads everything out for me. Everything from the items needed to the step-by-step instructions. Everything except the notes from my predecessors and the ratios, which we don't have. "I-Is there anything else?" I ask after a half hour of listening, despite having read it multiple times myself.

"Yes. There's quite a lot really. Some theories, or theorems as they're called here, and weird rants about spacetime and gravity and words I can't even pronounce."

"C-can you remind me of t-the first t-thing t-that is needed for t-the T-time Machine?" Probably the most important part of the whole thing has managed to slip my mind.

"The Sanium." Of course! Sanium. The problematic element. When I last tried to get a hold of some, I didn't get it, but something similar, which was probably what caused the... incident when I travelled to the past.

"W-we need t-to be c-careful with it." I say, recalling my previous experiences. "I-It can be dangerous and easily mistaken for something else."

"Ya think?" There is a hint of frustration in her voice. She knows it was the problem, even without either of us saying it aloud.

"C-can you reread t-the information about t-the different t-types of t-time."

Amethyst huffs and rummages through the papers as minute of two, takes a loud gulp of water and reads "One possibility is the Immutable timeline. In the immutable timeline events are believed to be fixed and unchangeable. Any actions taken do not have the power to alter the past, present or future. This is where the idea of fate comes from, bla bla bla. Next there is the Mutable Timeline. The mutable timeline allows for changes, meaning that choices affect the timeline. This is where the idea of free will is introduced. Lastly, there is Alternate Histories. Alternate Histories is linked with the concept of the multiverse, where there is a timeline for every major decision made." Amethyst takes a well-deserved breath after the amount of reading she did.

"S-so we're in either t-the Mutable or t-the Alternative Histories. R-right? S-since I changed the past, and t-the events in c-certain t-textbooks have c-changed."

"Most likely the Mutable T-timeline. What is the chance that there are millions of timelines, and they are hidden from us?"

"P-pretty high, but we c-can say we live in t-the Mutable T-timeline. T-that would mean t-that anything c-could happen, and t-that our future is not 'set in stone.'"

"Well, wow. What was the point of me reading all that out if that's the only conclusion you can make?"

"I-I want t-to make sure we are c-clear on every detail. E-even t-the small ones."

The chair beneath Amethyst creaks as she changes position. "Now what do we do? Where do we go from here?" There are so many questions, yet so little answers.

"I-I t-think we need t-to wait for me t-to g-get out of the hospital. W-we c-can't risk being overheard."

"Too late for that, mate."

"A-also." I try to ignore her snide comments, "We have to go all the way to go to the Carribean to get Sanium. I-It is t-the safest place t-to harvest it."

"I know that, dumbo. I just read it to you. But you're forgetting that we won't manage to get to the dumb Carribean. Especially with your new disability." The word 'Disability' punches my gut.

"S-so you rather t-that we'll risk our lives in Africa? T-that's c-closer. T-there's no Sanium mines in t-the Uk, so t-that's not an option."

"I know!"

"S-so tell me. W-where will we g-get t-the Sanium from?" She doesn't reply. Maybe she shrugs, but I don't see it. Papers rustle. A pen scratches the paper.

"How about Italy?"

"N-no. D-did you see the reports on it? T-the Sanium mines c-collapsed years ago! W-when my great grandfather was alive!"

"At least I didn't say Scotland." She would be dumb to say Scotland, as there are no mines there.

"O-ok. L-let's say we decide Italy. I-I have a few q-questions. H-how will we g-get t-there? H-how will we actually get the Sanium? A-and most importantly, how are you planning on funding this trip? A-and isn't it illegal for us t-to drive? W-will we have t-to t-take a bus everywhere?"

"You wanted to go to the Carribean. How were you planning on that?"

"I-I don't know!"

"You're right." Amethyst mumbles, "We'll need a lot of money..."

"W-we're not doing anything illegal."

"Okay." She practically sings it. She was planning on something illegal, wasn't she? "How about... we work at DrSer's!" The chair scrapes the floor, probably because she stood up. I realise she thinks it's a brilliant idea.

"H-how much do t-they pay? I-It's around eight pounds an hour, right?" I do the maths in my head. "I-If we worked two hours a day each." I start to mutter my calculations "O-one day would be t-thirty-t-two pounds a week would be a little over t-two t-ten..." If we'll need two thousand pounds, just in case, that'll be "T-ten weeks!"

"Ten weeks?! What? Do we even have ten weeks to wait?"

"W-we c-could squeeze it into eight."

"Right. How bad are the glitches." I let the question hover in the air and I try to picture the unnatural colors and shapes in unusual places.

"I-I would say... m-medium." But if we waited eight weeks...

"And we need to account for your blindness, and ya getting out of the dumb hospital. And GCSEs which are coming up. And I have to put dinner on the table."

"S-stop. I-I know it'll be hard. Y-you don't have t-to t-tell me again." I interrupt her.

"Wait. How did you get the 'Sanium' in the first place?" She asks as an afterthought.

"M-my family and I went on holiday t-to t-the Carribean, and I managed t-to sneak away for long enough t-to harvest t-the wrong thing."

"Eight weeks it is." She grabs my hand, and my stomach twists.

"W-what?" Oh, our plan.

"Shake on it. We'll get the money in eight weeks, then go to Italy." Suddenly the reality of it all hits.

"Y-you realise we may be unable t-to get t-to t-the Sanium?" New doubts flood my mind.

"We have to try. Do ya want to know that ya are the last human on Earth, and ya had the chance to save everyone, and ya didn't even try?"

"O-ok." I shake her hand. Done. Eight weeks. Two months. Fifty-six days. We can do this. We must.

"Why are ya still wearing those ugly glasses?" Amethyst asks and I slide my black, tattered glasses off my face.

"I-I don't know! I-I didn't know I still had t-them on!" She laughs, and I join in. Phew. Even if I have to go save the world, I like knowing that people don't change.

Chapter 8: Max

Date: March 10th, 2024

It's pouring. The stormy weather outside matches the mood inside perfectly. Amethyst (who I barely managed to convince mum to invite) sits opposite me, because she was one of the last people to see my grandma alive.

"Your grandmother seemed like a lovely woman." Amethyst says awkwardly in an attempt to comfort me, but I don't reply. She was not lovely. She was amazing: the most incredible person in my life. But Amethyst wouldn't know that; she only met her once, when she got into a fight with Alex's friends two Tuesdays ago and needed patching up.

Rex pants at my feet, rolling on them, and I rub his head. He only knew my grandma for a little while too, but they had gotten close within just one visit from her, and they clicked instantly. If I ever -I mean, when- I finish my Time Machine, I'll go back and hug her once more. I can't do anything to keep her around, though, because I can't prevent her from dying from old age. That's what the doctors said she died from, but she was in great shape and barely sixty-five.

"Max?" My head snaps up at the sound of my name. "Get dressed. We're leaving in ten minutes. Lock the dog in your room."

"R-rex." I remind dad that 'The dog' has a name, too.

"Sorry. Lock Rex in your room." I don't know who apart from me still needs to change in to funeral clothes, but it's on the tip of my tongue. I call for Rex to follow me instead. I'm sure grandma is shaking her head in heaven, muttering that we should be in bright colors if we're trying to honor her and her memory. The thought doesn't even bring a smile to my face, because she's gone. She was my beacon of light. I wish I had told her that I loved her that last day when she'd left after her first and last encounter with Rex and the blind version of me. She died the next evening.

I hear dad's footsteps as he leaves for the kitchen, and I head in the opposite direction to my bedroom. I don't spend much time here anymore because it's so hard to navigate the clutter without help and I don't want to end up in hospital again. I also am not keen about Rex destroying my eggshell collection when he's locked in here, though I wouldn't have to clean it up anyway. I lock Rex in the room and take the suit (which I have been assured is neat and very much black) to the bathroom to change.

I feel awkward and stiff as I sit listening to a speech about how much we'll miss Annabel Nightingale and how incredible she was. Two of my sisters are crying on my left, making me even more uncomfortable. I can't match their sobs to their identity, but I don't mind the guessing game to keep grandma off my conscience. Amethyst is on my right, as still as a statue, and as tense as me. She insisted on being here, and I don't know why. I can't believe that she actually cares about my grandma, but that would mean that she is here for me. But she always says she hates me, so it's equally impossible to believe.

Tears are shed, her corpse lowered (which I'm glad I can't see. I can imagine her shallow, pale face and empty eyes well enough) and everyone slowly leaves. Amethyst and I stay outside of the house, as everyone gets in, and sobs are muted when the door swings shut. We stand in the rain, getting soaked to the bone, and I want to dissolve into nothingness and let humanity end. That way, no one could experience loss again, and no one would feel this way. It would be mercy.

"Will I see ya at work today?" Amethyst says, breaking the silence. How can she think of work?

"N-no." I murmur loud enough for her to hear over the constant dripping of rain. "Y-you won't see me at school either." She should be at school, though.

One second passes. Two seconds pass. "Are ya ok?" I want to answer with some sassy sarcasm, but that's an Amethyst thing, and I don't have the energy.

I don't reply and simply walk into the house. I'm drenched, and the floor is turning into a pool, but I don't care. I don't care that mum will yell at me. I don't care about anything but sleeping the painful days away. In sleep, I can forget that I'm blind, I can forget that grandma is gone, and I can forget about Time and school.

According to Siri, it's only one pm, but I'm going to go to bed anyways. Surprisingly, no one stops me, not even Rex, who stays by my bed all day and into the night.

Listening to audiobooks soon becomes a habit of mine, and I rarely do anything for pleasure (books are simply a form of escapism for me, not joy). I'm also constantly exhausted from the endless cycle: school, work, food, sleep, Time, audiobooks. On repeat. A never-ending cycle.

Chapter 9: Max

Date: March 15th, 2024

One random day, Amethyst asks me a peculiar question as we sit in the attic. My head is leaning against the bed, and I am sitting cross-legged like in primary school when she speaks up after a long silence. "What could sixteen to nineteen mean?" I'm still in the worst mood, and I shrug it off, despite it pulling at my curiosity slightly.

"I-It's probably t-the t-time. O-or a ratio."

"How about Fe sixteen to S nineteen?"

"W-where are you getting this from?" I ask, my curiosity peaked. "A-and please stop speaking so mysteriously."

"I got it from the back of one of the plans," She says casually, "When I held it up to the light, I saw a faint trace of Fe sixteen to S nineteen." I know that she is mimicking the movement as paper crinkles somewhere above our heads. "Could it be the ratio of iron to sanium?" She says pompously.

"I-I think so. B-but you don't need t-to be so arrogant about it."

"Me? Never." She is always like this. But it is a breakthrough, and it doesn't matter that Amethyst is acting smug about it. And it's one of the last things we need, not including money. I supress a smile.

"Should we celebrate?" Amethyst asks.

"W-where? A-and shouldn't we save t-the world first? A-and shouldn't we save our money?"

"Don't worry so much. This is our time to celebrate. Because *when* we save the world." I'm glad she didn't say the if that hangs in the air unsaid. "We won't be together to celebrate. I'll be in the past."

"O-or I'll be in t-the future, depending on t-the perceptive." Amethyst makes a weird, 'pft' sound, as if she is unsure what to say. Even though it's

Amethyst who always knows what to say. And how to make it sarcastic.

"So where are we going?" She asks, though it was her idea to go somewhere.

"A-anywhere but DrSer's. I-I'm sick of that place."

"Yeah, me too." She snorts. "How about we go to the bookstore/coffee shop down the road?" Anywhere but DrSer's and the place I spent the most time with my deceased grandmother.

"Umm." I don't want to say no, but I don't want to say yes. What should I say which is neither yes or no? "A-are you t-trying t-to insult me?"

"How is that insulting? No. I want to read ya something, to make ya feel better about... well, everything."

"W-wait. I-Is t-the pitiless Amethyst being nice? T-to me? S-someone she hates?" She takes my disbelief as sarcasm.

"Shut your mouth or we're not going anywhere." She sounds rude, but think she is trying to be friendly.

"B-but you're t-the one who wants t-to g-go."

"Let's go." She stands up with lighting speed like she did when we first met.

"B-but we have French homework."

"Do ya want to go or not?" I grin, and Amethyst picks me up with one arm, as if I were as light as a feather. I hope she's reciprocating my smile.

We read (more like Amethyst reads to me) Shadows of the Cresent Moon by Seraphina Ravensong. I listen, captivated by her funny voices for a crazy long time. I manage to drink three luxury hot chocolates in the time, and Amethyst gets through countless glasses of water. I know people must be staring at us, and the waitress has come over so many times that maybe she suspects us of something. But we aren't doing anything wrong, not right now.

"And with that, he smiled and sat down, telling his story to his young daughters, who were ecstatic to listen." Amethyst concludes with a final flourish, finally putting the book down, and she cracks her joints unpleasantly. "I now really need the bathroom. If you'll excuse me." She proceeds to go to the toilet, and I stretch as I wait for my own turn to relieve myself after the book. During it I had even forgotten that I was listening to a story, and I felt like Alan himself, watching Eva in action. Just not when Amethyst got another water.

"Your turn, then we're going back to your house." I snap out of the fictional world as best I can.

I relieve myself as Amethyst puts the books away and as I exit the toilet, I almost bump into the waitress who must be carrying over a dozen glasses. "S-sorry." I stammer, but the waitress doesn't say anything and rushes away. I realise that I haven't even heard her speak all evening, and the only way I know she is a woman is her little high-pitched coughs. Why am I thinking so much about the waitress? I'm not like Alan.

"A-amethyst." I say, not quite sure which way to go. "W-where are you?" No reply. No car noise comes from outside. This is not right. After a minute, I understand that this is another 'Time Glitch' as we have started calling it. But, I can't do anything other than wait for the world to begin playing again. In the silent stillness, I knock over a bookshelf, and a squeak comes from the other room: the kitchen.

Shouldn't I be the only one experiencing this? I cautiously walk to where I heard the squeak, listening carefully.

"H-hello? W-who is it?" There is a quiet rustle in the corner of the kitchen. "Umm... W-waitress?" I don't know what else to call her, but I think that was her high-pitched squeal. No more rustling occurs, and there are no more sound effects quiet or loud as I knock a table over. She's gone. How did she manage to escape without me hearing her?

"Max. Don't tell me ya did that again?" Amethyst says as I wonder.

Chapter 10: Celestia

Date: Uknown

Uki and Zosia dress in their finest clothes for Her Young Majesty's coronation. It is to be a spectacular event taking place in the palace itself and is supposed to be the most memorable event to date. As they prepare, Uki and Zosia confabulate.

"Did you know it's to be the biggest event in the Deca Millenium?" Zosia asks, tightening Uki's tie.

"Is it because we have finally adopted the human system of Monarchy and we are getting our first

Queen today?" Uki replies sarcastically, and perfects her outfit, her mind a million miles away.

"Well, yes. But anyway, apparently, we'll be able to see the parade from our parqui later." Uki nods. A parqui is a little bit like a human garden or a neighborhood area, but a lot nicer, including everlasting Floras and a Meadow veil. Flors are quite like flowers and a Meadow Veil is something a human mind can't comprehend. To simplify it, it brings the user pure pleasure and is easy to get addicted to.

Zosia does a little spin, showing off her golden dress that spans across even more dimensions than Uki's suit and shines brighter than the stars Uki creates. *"Do you like it?"* Zosia pouts.

"I love it."

"Really?"

"Yes. Definitely." Zosia's eyes turn the same gold as her dress and as sparkling as her six gloves whilst her happiness blows up.

"I know." Zosia knows everything. She *is* wisdom herself.

Human-style music plays outside. *"We need to hurry! We can't be late! Achiles is waiting for me!"* Zosia exclaims. Of course he is. He is one of the only ones Zosia had not used the Meadow Veil por deux with. We float outside to see the parade starting. Colours spanning from Rapture to Willow to Mist stretch as far as Uki can see. Dancers and singers and actors shout and move about as we head towards the palace, where the parade has not yet reached. Loud music plays from somewhere, and each dimension is filled with pure joy. Confetti falls from the sky, and glitter litters the floor.

In the palace, Achillies swishes Zosia away towards the dance floor the second they enter, spinning Zosia around. But Uki stays a moment to observe the intricately carved doorway and lines and lines of food. "Food..." Uki mutters under her breathe like a human who has been starved for weeks. Uki has never had food before.

Uki wonders what the monarchy will do after giving up their throne, since they have forever ahead of them.

She spots Horace in the distance, and Uki realises this is the first time she has seen Horace in public without Morana. Horace looks smart for the wicked Celestial he is, with his back turned, and malicious eyes hidden. But as he looks round, he can't hide the empty eyes and black-hearted intentions for they are clear as a human's day. He locks eyes with Uki and she ducks away to devour some food. The fatty delicacy melts as she eats it, and the new sensation would make her giddy if she hadn't seen Horace. She tries some crunchy treats that are like punches in the face and some heart-warming, slightly pungent bronze squares. What else have the humans invented? She tries some cubes of gently damp material which is pleasant to try.

"What a fine *buffet* this is." Horace says and makes Uki jump. He is one of the only Celestials who uses standard words and not minding. Morana had told him that she preferred it that way. If Uki had a stomach, it would have churned. Morana may never be back because of Max, and Horace knows it too. He's not to blame for trying to get her back.

"It is." She doesn't turn around. She can't look. Every glimpse of him makes her sick. *"And I will be off to enjoy the other activities now."*

"I am sure you will survive a minute talking to me, instead of those *giftless* ones." Giftless Celestials are often treated as worse, despite there being barely any Gifted ones. Very few Celestials are

Gifted. Uki (who is gifted and not permitted to become human) would rather listen of the tales of being on Earth than talk to Horace. She helped create it, after all, but it would be unacceptable for her to go.

Uki nods. If she doesn't say yes to Horace, the coronation will seem to fly faster than a human eagle thanks to his powers. "Great." Horace spins her round to face him and carefully picks the words he says. "I need to ask for... a favour. You see, Valda didn't do what I asked." Valda? Does this have something to do with his beasts? "And I think you are the only other being who could do this... favour." Uki is in control of space and dimensions. What could Horace want with those?

"What do you want me to do?" The room gets more and more busy as it nears the crowning ceremony.

"You know how you can change the dimension you're in..." It's not a question nor a statement.

"Yes." Uki starts to feel wary.

"I need my pets to meet the third dimension." No. No, no, no. "What do you say about a Saturday meeting? We could get some human food too..." He wants to kill Max. Uki has spied for Horace before but has never been involved with killing. She will never willingly take someone's human life away.

"Umm."

"Don't worry." He whispers, "You don't have to answer now. Just show up. Or don't. Your choice." Horace glides away and finishes with minding. *"Remember what I can do."* Uki had never heard Horace's mental accent before. No wonder Morana wanted him to use his other voice. Suddenly, Uki's body collapses in on itself and she falls to the floor, struggling to handle the searing pain. She wants to yell at Horace, but she is weak with agony. To prevent embarrassing herself, she nods. What can she do? She has to do as he says.

If Valda didn't listen to Horace, then what has he done to her? There is no way she succumbed to his call: she has always been stronger than Uki. As the tension in her starts to relax, she regains sight she had not realised she had momentarily lost. The ceremony starts.

"Ladies and Gentlemen," A familiar voice sounds in Uki's head. *"This is Oba minding. Welcome to my dear daughter's coronation."* Anger punches Uki's still-churning Xavil. The Kings and Queens from now on will be able to have children, and even Gifted Celestials like herself can't even do the human act.

What's worst is that Uki will have to send them into the third dimension to do it, but she will never be able to experience being a mother, all because of the stupid society standards. It's even worse since she will never see the planet she sends so many to. At least, not from a normal human perspective. Uki pushes all the thoughts down, as she always does. As she must. She cannot die, but she can feel eternal pain if she ever says her ideas aloud.

Uki soon realises that she missed half of Oba's speech because of her thinking. *"I pronounce you, Gina Heather, Queen of the Celestials!"* The crowd cheers aloud. It's incredibly loud and joyful since this is the biggest event since humans were created. And that was over three thousand years ago.

The new queen says a few words of her own, and Uki's jaw would have dropped if she had one. Queen Gina wears gorgeous robes of every colour in the two hundred and seventy-one dimensions, and every millimetre she moves, a new colour seems to appear. Her face is perfect, her eyes matching her robes like most of the women. But most incredibly of all, she has long, golden hair. Most celestials don't decide to have hair, so remove it from their profile. And those who keep it, keep it short. She's so uniquely stunning, that Uki's hands shake slightly.

"I hope all of you, dear citizens, are having a good time." The crowd is more enthusiastic this time round. *"I am overjoyed to be your Queen. During my reign, I promise to listen to all your needs and requests. Even the requests of the ones with no gifts."* That's new. *"And I have much in store for you, my dear Celestials. I am excited to be working with you and for you."* Uki is amazed by the new Queen's boldness and confidence. She looks so small and fragile as she takes her father's hand and walks down from the make-shift stage.

Uki knows Oba well, because she has been helping him since the day he and his soulmate were the Celestials chosen to have a child. A Ruler. Gina. The last time Uki saw Gina, she was smaller than Uki's arm, and a little wailing thing. That moment when Uki held the baby Gina was Uki's only taste of motherhood. And now Gina is an adult, and a Queen.

Someone taps Uki on the shoulder, and she jumps up in surprise. "Uki?" The young Queen whispers.

Eyes wide, Uki feels hot and shakes Gina's hand. *"Your Majesty."* She bows awkwardly. *"How do you know my name?"*

"My daddy told me all about you." Her eyes are bright, and her hair is gorgeous. Uki wonders whether she should grow out her own hair. "He told me you would be able to help me make my dream come true."

"What is that, Your Highness?"

"You'll find out tomorrow. You must come find me, and you'll help me. Yes?"

"It would be my honour." Her mind races. What could this be about? *"I shall see you later."*

"Bye!" She waves, in a manner Uki would imagine a little girl to wave in.

⧗

Uki pokes her head round the corner, looking for Gina hopefully. But she is not there- of course. She's too busy being Queen for human problems. Uki shakes her head and takes her place.

"Is everyone here?" Morpheus asks, addressing the small group. His eyes scan over where the Queen would be sitting and gives Uki an appreciative nod, which she returns. *"Almost. So, who has any updates about project Earth? Zosia, you first."* Project Earth are Celestials on a mission to help Max and Morana save the first humans, in order to save all of humanity. In the group there is five of them: Uki, Zosia, Valda, Morpheus and Xander.

"Well, I know that Max and Morana are back on Earth and are making The Time Machine as we speak."

"Brilliant. Uki?"

"I know that Horace is fuming. He's lost three Tilons and has started attacking Earth Time. He's made me spy for him and probably many humans are at risk, if not all of them."

"What do we do about it?" Xander makes his hands into fists, readying for a fight.

"That's not everything." Valda sings. *"He has created a chain of threats, including the Queen herself."* Uki fidgets nervously at the mention of Gina.

"Let's beat Horace up then." Xander storms towards the door but is held back by Zosia. He groans slightly as her fingers dig into his back.

Uki explains, *"If we hurt Horace, we hurt the human timeline, which won't make Max's and Morana's job any easier."*

Xander huffs, breaking free of Zosia. *"Then what are we going to do?"*

Morpheus replies, his eyes bright, and his hands playing with mini clouds and stars. *"When they're ready, we'll give them some prophecies that'll lead them in the right direction, and for now, we'll try and convince those in the 'chain of threats' to not listen to Horace."* The group nods in approval and disperses soon after.

Uki hopes that Horace won't hurt anyone just to get Morana back.

Chapter 11: Amethyst

Date: March 17th, 2024

"Why are we studying for a stupid exam, when we are about to go on a time-traveling, leave-everything-behind trip?" I ask Max, my head dangling off the bed I've been occupying on the nights we stay up too late.

"I-If we succeed, we should be back in t-time t-to t-take our G-GCSEs." Max sits, simply thinking since he can't see the plans or study guides, and I have forbidden him from drawing his chicken scratch all over them.

"Mhm. If we succeed, I won't be here." I flip the right way up, my head heavy from the blood rushing from it.

"T-true. T-that's why you're not doing anything." His hand feels around the empty spot of floor.

"Pen?"

"Y-yes. P-please." I hand him a pencil to feel as if I am disobeying him, even if it's just a little.

"By the way, I am doing something. I am doing all the writing for the both of us."

"Y-you're t-the one t-that doesn't let me write on *my* plans!"

"Yeah, 'cause I wanna be able to read what is written, and your writing is worse than a toddler's!"

"I-I'm sure it's not that bad."

"Trust me, it is." I laugh, then slap my mouth over my face. I have to be serious. Max is not my friend. I'm not to laugh with him. I'm not to *enjoy* my time with him, even if we have bonded on multiple occasions.

He smiles gently. He better have gotten the impression that I hate him. I do hate him. He ruined my life. TWICE.

"W-what did you hit?"

"Nothing. A... fly. So, like I was saying, we shouldn't be wasting time studying math theorems we'll never use, but doing work, earning money, perfecting our plan!" Before I know it, I'm on my feet, as if I'm giving a motivational pep talk.

"I-It's not like we c-can set off t-tomorrow."

"We might have been, if we spent more time on it." I slump back down on the bed, the springs creaking beneath me.

"Y-you c-can g-go t-to work now, if you wish."

"I might as well." I stay where I am.

"P-please don't."

"Clearly, I'm not going anywhere." Unfortunately. "Now, what did ya want me to read?"

"N-never mind. I-I remembered how t-to do it." He closes his notebook clumsily. "I-If you want, you can go home."

"Are you trying to kick me out? No *thank ya*." I do hate Max, but I hate being home even more than being around him. The questions. Mum's immaturity. The broken walls. The list goes on. "But actually, I would like to go to work." A busy mind is a happy mind.

"W-why are you so desperate t-to g-go t-to work? W-we have all t-the money we need. A-and t-they're t-tired of us working overtime almost every other day."

I swing my bag over my arm. "They'll just have to deal with me. I have nothing better to do, and we can't be sure of anything." "W-would you feel better if we ordered our plane t-tickets?" I plop the bag and stare at him, knowing he can't see my rapidly growing grin. I understand where this is going.

"Yes. Very much yes." I drop down opposite him.

"O-open my phone. T-the password is one, one, one, one."

"So safe." I say sarcastically, as I pick up the phone and use his face to unlock it. Why should I be bothered with the password?

"A-and t-turn on g-google." He ignores my comment.

"I know how to order plane tickets, thank ya very much."

"O-ok." The clicking of the phone is unnaturally loud.

"So now what?"

"Y-you said you know how t-to order plane t-tickets." I roll my eyes. "A-anyway, we order a flight. F-from London, t-to Milan Malpensa airport."

"Ya got this figured out, haven't ya?"

"Y-yeah. Y-you're not t-the only one who wants t-to g-get g-going." My stomach flips. It's weird to think that Max and I might have something in common.

"The soonest flight is for the thirtieth of March."

"H-how much is it?" We're doing it.

"One hundred and fifty-seven pounds per person."

"C-click 'book', t-then 'two persons', and lastly 'c-confirm."

"Clicked, clicked, and clicked." Silence. It's happening. It has been booked.

"G-good. N-now help me g-get downstairs. I-I still have house c-chores t-to do." He sounds like an old man. As we exit, Rex comes up to us, and licks Max. "G-good t-to see you, t-too." He smiles in a way that would enchant a girl, if he were anyone other than himself.

⧗

I arrive home early compared to most days. So early, that mum is not yet asleep. What a shame. "Amethyst! Where have you been?" She crushes me in an embrace. This is first time I've seen her in maybe three days. At least, whilst she is conscious.

"I was over at Max's. I've told ya before."

"Is that the blind boy?"

"Yes." Surprisingly, it feels weird calling him 'the blind boy', as it's not the first thing I think about him, and I met him when he could still see. This may make me sound weak, but I feel sorry for him, being known only for what he doesn't have. But I'll never tell him that.

"Amethyst?" Did I zone out thinking about Max?

"Yes?"

"I was asking what's for dinner." I'd forgotten that there wasn't much in the fridge.

"I already ate with the Mangas."

"What about me?" Her chubby face droops.

"There should be soup in the fridge..."

"I already finished it all."

"Do ya want jacket potato?"

"Yes!" Her face brightens again.

"Go do something, it should be ready in two hours." Mum goes off pouting that she's hungry and doesn't want to wait, but my mind is focused on the flight. I'll be leaving my foster mum forever. She'll have to do everything herself again. I let the potatoes bake as I do the chores I'd been neglecting for days. I don't change into my comfy clothes, as I have left them at Max's. Again. I'm losing my head with all of this monotonous planning. Time and time again, I get up still tired, go to school, then go to Max's, go to work, then come home late to chores and a moany or sleepy woman. Every day. On repeat.

Maybe I should move in with the Mangas'; I would have just a few more minutes of precious sleep and less housework. Mum would crumble into pieces, but I'm leaving her one way or another; it'll be like a training session.

I head to my room and chuck stuff in my spare bag. I'll live in the attic and afford my own dinner. They'll barely notice. I'll be just another girl in the crowd of daughters.

I text Max on my cell phone, hopeful that he is alone in his room, so siri won't tell the whole world that I'm coming. 'Coming over now. Could I stay a few days?' I send the message.

A reply comes two minutes later, 'Yes, comm. Willy be happy two have u.' A smile crawls up my face. Max's siri doesn't send the most... accurate messages. I consider messaging back, but figure there's no point; I'll be at their house in four minutes. Maximum.

"Potatoe's in the oven. Just add some butter and cheese and it'll be good to go."

"Where are you going?"

"I um... forget something at Max's." How do you tell your adoptive mother that you're leaving her forever?

"You're being weird."

"No, I'm not." I give mum a quick hug and approach the door, adjusting the bag on my shoulder.

"Yeah you are. What are you doing there with Max?"

"Nothing. Just studying. For GCSEs and stuff."

"Are you sure?" She grabs my face and examines me, making me stutter.

"Y-y-yeah." Now I'm as pathetic as Max.

"Are you sure that you're not more than study buddies?"

"What? Oh. Ooh." My eyes widen. Is that what Max's parents and sisters think we are? "Umm." That's embarrassing.

"Mhm." Mum grins. "Mommy always knows. Are you having fun with him?"

"Y-yes. But I don't have much to compare it to..." I can't deny it: it is very suspicious that we spend so much time together. We spent a third of the half term in that attic.

"I'm so happy for you." She grabs my arm that holds my bag up. "What's in here then?"

"It's my," Think. Think! I'll tell the truth. Mostly. "It's my clothing. I will be with Max for a while. We wanna spend more time together."

"More? What a passionate romance you must have." I want to gag.

"Yeah." I back away, "Yeah. I gotta go. See ya." An afterthought hits me. "Remember to not eat takeaway food every day."

"Me? Take away food? Do you even know me?"

"I do." I force a chuckle. "Bye." I finally leave. The fresh air makes my head spin. Now my mum thinks that I am Max's girlfriend. How brilliant. What if she says that to Mrs. Manga? That would be destroy me.

Knock. Knock. Knock.

The door swings open. "Amethyst!" Mr Manga doesn't seem surprised to see me, only excited. "Max said we could be expecting you." He winks. I have not had many interactions with Max's father, but he seems like a good man. He's working most of the time to support his many children. "Come on in, unless you want my wife believing you have hyperthermia or something."

"Thank ya." I nod my head in appreciation, before Mrs. manga strides in.

"Did I hear that Amethyst is here?" She does a funny little shimmy.

"Yes, ya did." I inform her. I take my jacket off, relieved that I'm leaving its constrictions.

"Let me take that." She leaves my hands empty of my jacket and bag. "I will take it upstairs for you."

"Thank you." At first, Mrs. Manga treated me like a guest, then like a monster (due to the library, Max, blind incident.) and now she treats me like royalty. Or is this how a mother treats her daughter? Does she think of me as a daughter now? "Jack, take Amethyst's stuff upstairs." She shoves my stuff towards Mr. Manga. I head after him to the attic.

On the way, I come across Gemma, losing sight of Mr. Manga. Ugh. Gemma. "Hey, baddie." It's one of her overused greetings.

"Bye, snobby." I storm away. Once upon a time, I was hanging out with her boyfriend for like, ten minutes. And it was about our DT, which Max isn't in, so I couldn't ask him. So, I was talking to him and the next day he broke up with her and said it was because his brother died. It makes no sense, but now

Gemma has the idea I bring bad luck, because of what happened with Max. I don't! It's simply a creepy coincidence.

Next, I come across Gabriella. "Hey!" She runs up to me. "How are you? Good. Anyway, I need a bit of advice." She makes a kissy face, making her look like a duck. "I need advice on getting a guy's heart. Yes, I know. I'm five years older, I should know, but you are literally a master. I NEED to know your secret." She speaks so quickly it's hard for me to keep up. "Is it your kissing? Your fashion? BTW, your hair is soo cool. I bet that's it."

"Umm... I..."

"It's the sarcasm, isn't it? I'm too positive, aren't I? Thanks for the tip. I always knew it was my positivity!"

"What's up with me being the master of 'capturing a guy's heart'? I'm," I stop myself. Gabriella probably has the same impression as my mum. Wow. How am I just now realising how suspicious we've been? "Sure, you're right. And some extra advice is to talk slowly."

Gabriella grins, and salutes. "Yes, ma'am." She skips away. Will I also have to face Georgia, Ginny and Gizelle? Seriously, can't I be left alone?

Finally, I arrive at the attic, where Max is sitting by the lonely desk. "I-Is that you, Amethyst?" He asks, swivelling around on his chair.

"Who else? Dummy." On the floor below, I can hear Gemma and Gabriella arguing. I know it's them because one voice keeps saying that I am a bad luck charm, and the other keeps telling it that I'm the best with men. How ridiculous.

"I-Is that... G-gemma and G-gabriella? F-fighting over you?"

I roll my eyes, "Yep."

"T-they are seriously running out of t-things t-to disagree about. A-and since when have you had a boyfriend?" I flush, the room suddenly too hot, and too small.

"Everyone is under the impression that we... ya know. The time we spend here together is... weird." Amethyst! Why are you being so weak? Toughen up! "No surprise really."

"T-they t-think we are a couple?" He doesn't sound as shocked or disgusted as I would like him to be. He seems like he's confirming something, and not questioning it.

"Even my foster mum said it." I get the idea to actually sit down and get ready for bed. It must be ten, if not later. "Max?" He's gone very quiet.

"W-will you t-tell t-them we're not... y-you know."

"What other reason do we have to be spending hours at a time together?"

"Y-you're g-going t-to let t-this idea stay?"

"Yeah, basically." Is that such a shock to him?

"Y-you won't beat my family up for thinking it?" I laugh. His face! He looks terrified!

"Do ya think I fight my way out of every situation?"

"N-no."

"That's a lie."

"I-I'm not afraid of you."

"I never said you were." He totally is.

I realise Mr Manga still has my bag of clothes. As if choreographed, there is a knock at the door. "Come in."

"Ok. Are you guys ok?"

"Yes. We're fine."

"Well, I have your bag Amethyst."

"Just leave it by the door please."

"Sure thing." When I am sure he is gone, I pick it up and change.

"W-why were you so rude?" Max asks.

"I wasn't." I fall into bed and sink into the blankets.

"I-If you say so. C-could you g-guide me t-t-to my bed? P-please?" I groan and grudgingly get up and give him my arm. "T-thanks." When he seems comfortable, I head back to my bed and lie down, my head swimming with thoughts and fears and hopes. I sigh. It's a lot to think about and digest, but at least we are heading towards the end goal.

"A-are you ok?"

"Me?"

"Y-yes."

"I'm fine. I think."

"Y-you t-think?"

I am now his roommate. I can talk to him about stuff. "I'm nervous. I don't remember most of my life, I'm about to leave the country and my foster mum." I take a minute to think. "I've technically already left my foster mum, and the last thing I said to her was 'Bye'. Who says 'bye' when they are leaving their only family member forever."

"I-It's better t-than saying see you later, or hi." Imagine saying hi instead of bye.

"Maybe. But still, I'm worried about... everything. That it will all go wrong." I turn over in my bed, which feels as familiar to me as the one in my own house. The bed and house that I've left.

"M-me, t-too."

"I thought so. Ya look like someone who would be afraid of their own shadow."

"T-thanks?"

"It's not a compliment."

"Oh."

"Do ya think we have a chance?"

"Y-yes. B-but don't ask me how big t-the c-chance is, as I will probably t-tell you."

"Is that a joke?"

"D-did it sound like a j-joke?"

"A little," I smirk. Probably the most fearful, smart, and unhumerous person will be accompanying me on this journey. What a duo we'll make.

What a couple we make. I cringe. How can they believe I could love Max? I get him loving me. I am awesome after all, and I'm being very generous by helping him, but Max is like a fragile bird. One that could blow over in the wind. I don't think I could ever even fake feelings towards him.

"C-can I ask you a question?"

"Ya just did." I joke.

"C-can I ask you two questions?"

"Ya just did." This has played out perfectly, and I'm not going to waste the opportunity.

He huffs. "C-can I ask you four questions?"

"Ya already did."

"W-when?"

"Now."

"A-are you serious?"

"Five questions." Max stops talking. I personally thought it was funny. "What did ya want to ask me?"

"H-how you feel about who you are. Y-you know. O-one of the first humans on Earth and all?"

Why is he trying to get my guard down? I already said enough. I will not answer. I will not answer. He is too nosy for his own good. "I don't know." I snap. "Can we just, go to sleep?" I've already told him too much. He doesn't need to know more.

"S-sure. W-we need energy for school t-tomorrow." Ugh. School. Alex is such a pest, and helping Max around is so embarrassing. Everything about Max is embarrassing.

"Night," I say, and he gives a gentle snore in reply.

Tonight, I find it hard to fall asleep, and when I do, I can only dream of Max. I can't tell whether they're dreams or nightmares, though.

Chapter 12: Amethyst

Date: March 29th, 2024

I wake up with a start. Today is the day. "Max." I hiss. "Wake up." I roll out of bed and check my phone. It's only five twenty-five. "Never mind." I don't go back to bed but decide to go for a quick walk to calm down. Today is the day. We're leaving.

I get changed, considering how likely it is that someone else is currently up. Unlikely.

In the garden, I turn my phone flashlight on, and head to my favourite spot: the rose bush. The cool night air whips around me, making my pyjamas sway in the breeze. The sky is glittered with stars tonight, and the moon shines brightly. There is only one cloud as if heaven had decided to stay close to Earth for us tonight. To help me and Max?

I take a seat on the bench, not even looking around to see if anyone is watching; I know Mrs. Manga is.

Smiling to myself gently, I lean over and puck a rose from the bush, easily avoiding the thorns that could draw blood with a single touch. The though gives me an odd, pleasurable, desire. The darkness in me threatens to take over as it makes my fingers close around the rose sharply, making me bleed splendidly. It surges inside me, turning the rose to dust before my eyes in a matter of seconds.

I unclench my fist, and a little of the blood-dust mixture flows out through the spaces between my fingers. The rest of it I smear on half my face, a crumb entering my mouth unexpectedly.

That's when I snap out of my weird phase, scrubbing my face furiously as my tongue gets stained with the taste of blood and something burnt. I mentally beg for my scars from last time to not re-open as my breathing gets heavy. Why do I always lose control? I cough and drop to my knees next to my phone, which flashlight is still on, and my hand clumsily reaches for it.

I slam the ground with my fist then rise to sit on the bench again. I murmur the alphabet backwards, trying to calm myself. "C, B, A..." I open my eyes to the bright sunrise shining at me. It's too cold to stay outside. But I don't want to cross paths with Max's mum after my breakdown. My ears listen out for her as my eyes scan the golden and amber sky.

"Good morning, Mrs. Manga." I say as the door opens.

"Could you really call this morning? The sun is barely up."

"I am not sure. What are ya doing up so early, Miss?" I twist my face away from her so she doesn't see the blood and I clench my fist to hide my cuts.

"I could ask you the exact same."

"I fancied myself a walk in the garden." As I realise I sound like a Victorian lady, I cringe. "How about ya?"

"I saw you out here and was wondering whether you're ok."

"I'm fine."

"I would disagree." She comes to stand next to the bench, mimicking how fell to the ground. "You may not want to tell me, but I want to know what you did here." Her eye catches the ashes. When I don't reply, she changes the topic. "How did you make my only son fall for you?"

"I don't know." This seems like the only conversation people can have nowadays.

"You're Max's first." *First what?* I spit back at her in my head. She laughs. "Could I ask you a question?" Reminds me of my conversation with Max the other week. "What made you interested in Max." Now I'm on the spot. Is there even a positive quality that Max has? Apart from messing stuff up, but that's hardly positive.

"He's just so smart." I try to sound in love. "Kind, and sensitive." Yuck! What nonsense! How come I'm letting it come out of my mouth? "Something about him just makes me want to..." Want to... what? "Be around him."

"Don't let Max ever find out I told you, but I'm surprised you think that. He is quite," She pauses, pressing her lips together as she looks for the correct work, "Problematic at school."

I shrug. "I can't say he's not."

"Now, Amethyst, no need to be so polite."

"I wasn't being polite. I know he is bullied at school. I know he's different, but he's not half bad." He couldn't be a bad boy if he tried.

"I am overjoyed that Max has someone like you, who can defend and help him." Am I a bodyguard, or his girlfriend? On second thoughts, I would prefer to be his bodyguard. Mrs. Manga checks her watch. "It's best if you go wake Max now. I wouldn't be surprised if he still will be late." She waves me away and I take the hint to leave.

When I arrive in the attic, I find Max already up, patting my bed down as if it were a police search. "I'm here, sleepy head."

"G-good. I-I was afraid you had been k-kidnapped."

"Ya know I would have knocked them out in one blow." I make a sound affect to emphasise my point.

Max smiles weakly. "W-we're doing it."

"Yes, we are."

"B-but first..." He says, but I interrupt him.

"I need to give ya your clothes, pack your bag, and lead ya downstairs before school." I chuckle. "I know. We do this every day."

"I-I was g-going t-to say t-that we need t-to double c-check whether we have everything packed for t-tonight, but ok."

"We do need to do that, too." I notice that Max is still searching for something. "Your bag is here," I pass him the shockingly heavy bag.

"Come for breakfast!" Mrs. Manga calls us for our (my, I remind myself. Max will return.) second-to-last meal in this house. Maybe even the country.

⧗

"Just leave Max alone!" I yell in Alex's face. Being 6'2, I tower over him, but he still looks at me as if I were the short one. A crowd emerges from the depths of the canteen.

"Or what?"

"You're gonna get what's been coming for ya a long time." I snarl. "I will swat ya away like the little fly ya are."

"Ya, ya!" He mocks. "Ya, ya! Are you perhaps from Germany?"

He sticks his middle finger in the air. "Wow, that's very rude. But did you know that you are the reason God created the middle finger?"

"Sure, and you're the reason he said..."

"La, la, la. I can't hear you." I stick my fingers in my ears.

"What a perfect fit. Blind boy, and deaf girl. How romantic."

"Ya make me sick." I point towards the exit, "There is the door. On the other side, there is a lovely stick for ya to chew."

"What are you calling me?" He scrunches his nose like a bull, and I flash my metaphorical red flag at him.

"Nothing at all. I'm just suggesting that ya can go have a nice day... but somewhere else."

"All these words." He dramatizes. "Why don't you use those damm fists of yours already?" He shows me his.

"What a cute hypocrite. Ya won't hit me, will ya?" I spot Max in the corner, slowly spinning round in circles, trying to find where the action is coming from.

"You better hit me. I have a whole collection of embarrassing photos of Max I could send to the whole school if you don't."

"Sure, ya do." What a threat. Non-existent photos. This is getting tiring, let's speed this up. "Watch out!" I call and he turns. I grab his wrist and twist, making him whimper like a scolded pup. I kick him in the shin, sending him toppling to the ground with a loud crash. As he lies on the floor, I stand on him as one would stop a football. I only move my leg when I am sure I've beaten him enough. He groans as he slowly gets back on his feet.

He grins, "Thanks for that." He holds onto the wrist I almost twisted off.

"What for?" I smile smugly back at him.

"Look behind you." Oh no. I manage to hide my shock and concern by disguising it as confidence.

"Afternoon, Mrs. Manga." She looks so much like Max, the only major differences being that her hair is grey and her eyes are focused on me like on a target she's about to shoot.

"Afternoon." She pauses, her eyes flickering to Max for a split second. "My office, Miss Lopez." I don't head to her office, but towards Max and Alex.

I whisper into Alex's ear, "Good job, big boy." And he smirks, being too thick to understand that I'm being rude. I turn to Max, "Soon we'll be gone." He blinks stupidly, not quite in my direction, but close enough. Then a grin that I would say equals Alex's smugness spreads across his face. Clearly, he is relieved that I'm not going angry at him for getting in Alex's way. His glossy, unfocused eyes light up, like leaving Alex, at least temporarily, is better than any Christmas gift anyone could get. I agree.

"Hurry up." Mrs. Manga snaps. When I am close enough so that only I can hear, she adds, "Max better not be involved in this."

"It was mainly me."

She sighs. "Was it only this morning when I told you that I'm glad Max has found you?"

"Yes, ma'am" I reply seriously, and she thinks so hard it's visible on her face.

"Was that Alex? The one you hit." Who else?

"Yes, ma'am."

"Had he, Alex, been rude to Max again?"

"Yes, ma'am."

"And you were defending Max?" I would never defend Alex, not even in court.

"Yes, ma'am." I grin, seeing frustration growing on Mrs. Manga's face.

"Can you please stop saying that?"

"Yes, maaaaaa..."

She keeps talking before I have to think of something to say other that ma'am. We reach the office. "Then I stick by everything I said."

"What? Really?" I ask in half-disbelief as she opens the office door and I enter swiftly.

"You protected him, did you not?" She sits behind her desk.

"I guess." I copy her and take a seat.

"I still need to give you detention, for reputation's sake."

"I get that."

"Today, at three."

It's not a question, but I treat it as one. "When we come back from Easter half-term would be preferable to have the detention."

"I would ask why, but I may not wish to know." She's smiling sweetly like a little girl being let in on a big secret.

"Ya would most likely kill me if ya did." She nods, probably thinking about intimate things, when (in reality) we'll be slipping away late at night, right under her nose. Meaning, I won't manage to attend my detention at all, but Mrs. Manga does not need to know that.

She leans back in her chair, letting out a sigh, and tells me, "I'll let you go in a minute or two, to make it seem like I am listening to the whole story and such."

"Thank ya, Ma'am." I reply automatically.

She coughs and whispers, although there is no one else around to hear, "Should I do anything about that Alex kid?"

"Definitely." I whisper back, aware that the scenario isn't truly dramatic. This could have been happily ever after for Max and me, but we have a few chapters left in our story.

⧗

"Basically, your mum let me off with as little punishment as possible." I finish telling Max.

"W-why has she never been t-that nice t-to me?" Good question. *Maybe because you are a ridiculously nervous reck?* I shrug. "I-I am her son! A-and she lets you off?"

"Actually, she let me off because I was protecting ya. I already told ya."

"R-really?"

"Really."

"S-she does c-care for me?" "She would have kicked ya out a long time ago if she didn't." I say bluntly.

"W-why didn't you simply t-tell Alex t-that we're not... y-you know?"

"It wouldn't have made a difference anyway. He wouldn't believe me." Second time he's asked this. Does he think I like him or something? "Now go do your chores, and I'll set the table, unless you want to be grounded."

"B-but we're leaving in about eight hours."

"Exactly. We don't want to give your mum a reason to keep an eye on us tonight."

"W-will you help me?"

"When have I not?" I roll my eyes.

"When are you going to make it official?" Mrs. Manga asks as I try and eat my dinner, my stomach doing backflips in anxiety and excitement.

"Excuse me?" I look up from my roast chicken.

"You are silly," She looks from me to Max and back to me again. "We talked about this earlier. Your realtionship." Deary me, who knew dinner could go so wrong? Clearly it was coming for us, but I thought we would escape from it. What to say now?

"W-we, uh." Max stammers.

"No need to be shy." Mr Manga adds with the third wink of the night. "Me and your mum met even earlier than you two." Why does he wink at Max when he can't see him?

"And how did that turn out for you? A bucket full of children, that's what." Little Ginny informs him.

"Shush now, girl." Mr Manga tells Ginny, waving his hand in her face.

"I'm telling you. They're too young."

119

"Y-you're younger t-than us, G-ginny." Max exclaims and I sigh mentally.

"I know. Sometimes I forget due to how immature you are, but I know your age and my age, and I can do the math." She adjusts her ponytail as if preparing for a fight.

"Listen to your father, Ginny." Mrs. Manga looks tired, and I don't know why. Maybe work? Maybe Ginny? "As I was saying, you are such a cute couple!" I kick Max under the table, wishing I could show him with my eyes that I want him to say something instead of me. But I know he would be too shy anyway.

"We wanted to do it soon, but ya beat us to it!" I say overly enthusiastically. I can do this, just act super in love. Ew. I can't.

"It was not much of a secret." Mrs. Manga uses her husband's signature move: the wink. I look at Max in what I hope is a lustful way, and she giggles. GIGGLES! I want to slide down my seat, onto the floor, and through it, so low I could say hi to all the dead bodies in the graveyard.

Gabriella whispers to Gemma, not-so-discretely, "I helped them. I gave Max some gum that night when she first came over." What has that got to do with anything? I want to scream that they're wrong, and that I couldn't fall for Max, even if a drank a gallon of magical love potion.

We sit in silence for a long while, with me and Max looking down at our food –well, Max is simply pointing his head down, but same thing. All of his family is beaming, as if I'm the only partner they have met. Surely Gemma, Gabriella and Georgina and the other older ones have had a boyfriend before (I'm almost sure two of them are already married). Ah. I'm another girl to add to the collection, aren't I?

"I-I'm done." Max claims, and I copy him, saying the same.

"Put the dishes in the sink, Amethyst. Max will clean them up." Says Mrs. Manga.

"I can help him..."

"No." Her voice is unnecessarily sharp. "You go have a nice nap or something. I need a chat with my son." Is he in trouble now? I nod. How can I make it convincing that I will hate spending time away from him? Not a kiss. Not a kiss. Max looks like he has the same idea as he turns round, his arms flailing, trying to find me.

"Don't." I whisper into his hair when he grabs onto my waist. I freeze.

"Y-you're t-the one who wanted t-to k-keep t-this idea around." He whispers back, and holds onto my face, measuring out where my lips are. I want to punch him, and crush his face, but that would blow the whole act.

"Please. It's not necessary." I gulp. Ignoring me, he stands on his toes and I lean towards him. He pecks my lips gently. Heat floods my chest, and a shiver runs down my spine. I have never even touched a boy before and I don't even know how to kiss, but I give him a peck too. I hope it'll be convincing enough. I could collapse from the exchange right here and now.

My heart is still pounding when I fall onto my bed. He didn't have to do that. I could have been kept oblivious to the fact that he wanted to do it. I could have... I could have a lot of things, but now my mouth is stained with Max's strawberry-tasting lips forever. Forever and ever and ever. I want to cry. I want to yell. I want to run away.

I jump up, leaving my state of stress. I AM running away. Never again will I have to do that. But I did it once, and it'll never be undone. Technically it could, if we succeeded with the time machine etc. No. When we succeed. Not if. *It was nothing*, I convince myself. *All a show. A show that has made Max a permanent part of my life. Not only my life, but my soul! His DNA is going to be stuck on me forever!* "Stop having a mental breakdown!" I yell at my reflection in the mirror. "And get some sleep!" I roll into bed, fed up with everything.

When I'm sure that my alarm has been set for 1:35, I let myself relax and fall asleep. I thank everything that I'll be leaving this place tomorrow.

⧗

Chapter 13: Max

Date: March 30th, 2024

When I finally reach the attic, it is filled with snores. "H-hey, Siri." I whisper, "W-what t-time is it?"

"It is eleven forty-seven, Maximus." Siri's voice rings in my ears, despite it being muffled by my bag in which it is packed. Why did mum have to use a voice that sounds eerily like hers? It just brings back the words, 'But one wrong move, and you're out.' Out where? She wouldn't leave me on the streets. I am her son. I am not sure whether that means anything to her, though. I don't know, and I may never find out.

"H-hey Amethyst." I whisper in her general direction. I can't say it when she's awake, but I can't say nothing at all. "S-sorry for t-that," It's hard to say kiss aloud, even when I know she's asleep, "Y-you know what. I-I know I didn't have t-to do t-that. I-I know I'm selfish. B-but I wanted it- us." What's the point? It won't undo my actions. And she kissed me back. Kind of. She couldn't have *hated* it. There was nothing to it on her end. No emotion. No love. She must know that it's her fault, in a way. She was the one who wanted to keep this charade up, so I have nothing to say sorry for. I wish I could tell her that to her face.

When I'm ready, I snuggle into bed, determined to get some sleep in before we leave. "N-night." I mutter to myself beneath my breath.

Less than two seconds later, I'm steering a cart: the cart of doom. Around me brilliantly bright blue merges with the inky blackness. Silhouettes of people emerge from the blinding aqua, along with horses, then battlefields, then crowns. It all goes by too quickly for me to see in detail, but judging by the slithers I see, I know that it worked, and that I managed to time travel. For what seems like a long while, I go around twists and turns until my eyes feel like they're bleeding from the lights.

All too soon, I see a pure empty end, like a black hole that threatens to suck me in. I pull back the break and it squeals horribly. To my relief, I'm not quite at the end, as I'm not sure I want to see what happens if I went to before the beginning of time. But before I can take a breath, I have left the tunnel, and am falling to a deserted planet.

There are no trees. There is no water. There are no people. Or so I think at first. As I stare into the distance. Adjusting my glasses slightly, I spot a group of people. But I can't tell how many there are, because a massive fire is blocking my view of them. "H-hello?" I call out, stupidly thinking they may be able to hear me so far away. I start running towards them. They might need help. I don't know what I could do, but I still might be helpful. "H-hello?" This time the fire seems to shrink, and a figure turns in my direction. Behind the crimson and gold flames, I see girls. Six of them. "D-do you need help?" I am panting now, since I've never been the sporty kind.

"Who are you?" A voice penetrates my ears. The fire is now gone, and I can see that they look highly unusual, as if someone had designed them based on different colours. The girl with violet and black braids approaches me without any caution. "I asked you a question!" She grabs my collar, and all politeness is gone.

"I-I'm..." I start, but she disappears, and the world turns to squares of green, lavender and black. Music plays somewhere in the distance. Then everything is gone: I can no longer see anything.

⧗

"Max!" I feel my clothes sticking to my skin from sweat. I haven't had that nightmare in weeks, but it has shaken me as much as it always does.

"A-amethyst?" The dream had been so vivid, so much that I thought that I would be able to see when I open my eyes. "W-what t-time is it?"

"Who cares? We're late."

"L-late? W-where?" It takes a minute for my brain to remember. "O-ok. I-I'll j-just g-grab my bag..."

"I've already chucked it in the taxi." She yanks me out of bed. "Let's go."

"B-but, I'm still in pyjamas." I stammer as I trip down the stairs.

"No, you're not. Ya slept in your day clothes. Come on!"

"D-don't wake the house."

"Too late."

"W-what do you mean?"

"I saw your mum and dad in the kitchen." Cool night air punches me as we leave the house.

We sprint.

"H-have t-they noticed us?"

"Not yet. But they have noticed the taxi. Get in!"

"I-I can't see." I trip over my feet.

"I know." She stuffs me into the back seat like a dirty jumper into the wash basket and jumps in next to me. Luckily, the driver barely looks at us twice at us before pulling out of the driveway. For a split-second, I can hear Rex whimpering sadly and my heart is stabbed with guilt.

"Maximus!" Mum yells from the house, "Come back here!" as she trips over Rex and curses. She says that she wishes she never had a son. My eyes well up. Amethyst asks for the driver to turn up the radio, "I shall never call you my son again..." Her voice is lost in the song 'Party in the USA'. In perfect synchronization, Amethyst and I slump into our seats and sigh.

This is so ironic: mum just told me how she'll kick me out at any sign of trouble and I'm running away. Did she know? I think about my sisters waking up in the morning to me being gone. "I-I t-think it would be best if we t-turned off our location tracking on our phones." I want to kick my family out of my head. I want to be able to never look back.

"Already done that."

"C-can you help me then?"

"I already did it for ya too."

"H-how?"

"Ya told me your passcode, silly."

"O-oh, yeah." My brain still feels fuzzy from my nightmare. We sit in silence, Amethyst clicking something (which I presume is her phone) whilst I think about my dream. Even though Amethyst doesn't know about her past, I know that she's kept her personality. It's weird to think that I know what her world looks like, but she doesn't. Technically, it's our world, but a long, long time ago. But since she lived such a long time ago, how old is Amethyst? She must be ancient. Jesus, I kissed a woman who's thousands of years old.

"We'll be there in a half hour." The driver informs us, and Amethyst grunts in disapproval. "Sorry, Miss. But there is terrible traffic ahead. If you had been listening to the radio, you would have heard that there are some weird animals blocking the road. Codswallop, if you ask me." How long have we been in the car? It feels like it has been two minutes, but it must have been at least twenty.

"Good thing I didn't ask." She retorts. "And yes, I have been listening to the radio." So, I'm the only one who didn't. Will someone fill me in on this? Then she whispers in my ear. "I did a bit of research, since I couldn't believe it, and some eyewitnesses are saying they are beasts the size of elephants but look like a mixture of a tiger and a lion."

"W-wow. S-sounds like something straight out of a movie."

"I know. What's weirder is that no one saw them enter the city. One minute they weren't there, the next they were. Poof. Like a magic trick."

"Deary me, mates. You really need to learn to whisper."

"And you need to learn to not eavesdrop."

"Pardon me for listening in on the most exciting thing of the century. And in case you wanted to know..." We don't find out what we want to know, as suddenly the car spins a one-eighty before crashing into a tree with tremendous force. Luckily, I fall onto the Amethyst as the car hits the tree on my side. I hold my mouth to make sure I don't vomit from the momentum. Thank God I forgot to do my seatbelts, or else I would be a pile of flesh and shattered bones.

I clamber off Amethyst as she pushes me off, rummaging for something noisily. Outside, sirens ring: police cars. Or maybe ambulances. There's screaming, too, though not right outside. That means we've been knocked out of the chaos.

"W-what's happening?" I ask, slightly terrified. Footsteps like a giant's rumbles outside.

"It's the beasts." She whisper-shouts. "How on topic!" There is both excitement and fear in her voice.

"N-not right now. H-how big are t-they?"

"The size of elephants, like your friend said. And yes, I am ok, thanks for asking." The driver pitches in. If only I could see.

"Shush, both of you." Amethyst slaps my arm. "They're getting closer."

"Y-you're k-kidding."

"She is not."

"I said shush!" I hear the door open and Amethyst huffing as she clambers out. "Follow me!"

"I-I can't see you!" I yell for what feels like the thousandth time within the last two months.

"Goodness," She pulls me by the arm, out of the car, and onto metal railing. I tumble onto the ground.

"Yow!" I scream as she almost yanks my limb off, but she keeps pulling me, forcing me to stumble to a stand.

"Did I not say shush enough?" We run onto soft earth (grass). Amethyst suddenly lets go.

"N-not now!" I have no clue what's wrong with her, but she needs to get her head back in the game. "W-we'll t-talk about whatever you're feeling later if you want, because right now you have t-to drag me where we have t-to g-go, unless me becoming a pancake by a mythical beast was a part of t-the plan t-that I forgot."

"I said shush." She sounds happy, not angry now. She grabs a hold of me again and we run off. Something heavy lands before us, and the force nearly knocks me off my feet, but I grip onto Amethyst for stability.

Roars and shrieks fill the air, and I suddenly feel Amethyst relax. Oh no. I drop down to the ground as my hand which was holding Amethyst starts to tingle and burn. "D-damn A-amethyst." A gut feeling keeps me pinned to the ground as something of immense force lands. A burnt smell hits my nose as a hand lands on my shoulder.

"Max." Amethyst. "Let's go."

"W-what happened."

"Later." I obey and take her hand so she can lift me from the soggy mud. Disgusting.

We run. More like Amethyst runs and drags me along. But soon, the beasts' footsteps grow quieter. I am panting extremely hard by the time Amethyst decides we're far away enough to slow to a walk. Leaves rustle all around me, and I presume we are in some sort of forest.

"I-is the driver here? A-and how c-close are we t-to t-the airport?" I don't dare mention what happened.

"No, and we're here."

"O-our stuff!"

"I have my bag, and we have our phones. That's enough. We'll buy anything we need."

"D-do we have water?" The not-so-long run-for-our-lives made me horribly thirsty.

"I said we'll buy anything we need."

"O-ok." Amethyst doesn't let go of me for even a second as we enter the airport, making my hand feel numb from the lack of blood. But I feel safe with her death grip on me. Chatter in many languages floods my ears, and the twists and turns don't allow my brain to recall how to get back in case anything happens, and we get separated.

"W-when's our flight?" I ask.

"Three sixteen."

"I-I know. W-what t-time is it now?"

"Two fifty-eight." She snaps. Ok. I'll be quiet.

"W-were t-the c-creatures frightening?" I say softly.

"No. We ran for the fun of it." Her hold loosens the tiniest bit, either from relaxing a little, or getting annoyed with me. I hope it's the first.

⧗

When we land, Amethyst is in an even worse mood, shouting instructions at me, and slapping me when I do something wrong. She doesn't slap me hard, but it still stings. In the hotel, she doesn't even talk to the receptionist, and I have to ask a member of staff to lead me to our room.

"W-what's t-the matter?" I ask Amethyst when we are finally alone.

"Nothing." She mumbles. "I told ya already. I'm fine."

"Y-you don't seem fine." I press on, picking a bed.

"Ya can't see me." I want to tell her 'Well Done' for catching up with the times, but I figure she'll get even moodier.

"I-I c-can hear you, t-though."

"Congrats. At least ya can do something." She shoves me off the bed I decided to lay on, and I roll onto the floor painfully.

"I-It's not my fault t-that I c-can't see." I get back up and use the other bed.

"Then whose is it?"

"T-the driver's." I tell her stubbornly. We sound like two little kid arguing a petty argument. How are we supposed to save the world? "Y-you can tell me anything, you now."

"I can't. You're a boy"

"A-are you being sexist?"

"Ya just won't get it!" She cries. I hear springs from the mattress screech from under Amethyst's weight, telling me that she jumped onto the bed. "You're too stupid!"

"I-I am t-the first person ever t-to t-time t-travel." I remind her.

"And you're the reason we're stuck in this whole mess!" I feel a strong sense of de ja vu.

"W-would you have preferred t-that we never met?"

"Yes, actually." Not shocking. I think everyone feels like that way any me, but it still breaks my heart a little.

"I-Is t-this about what happened back at t-the c-creatures?"

"I told ya to shut it."

"F-fine. S-sorry for wanting t-to know. S-sorry for t-trying t-to be... b-be... c-caring."

"I don't need no care from ya."

"I-I disagree."

"Shut up, ya damn idiot!" That silences me.

"H-hey siri." I ask my phone. "W-what t-time is it?"

"Seven thirty-four, Maximus." How has it only been five and a half hours since we left my house?

"I-I'm g-going t-to have breakfast before I have a nap."

"Good for ya."

"I-I was wondering whether you want anything?"

"If I did, I would get it myself. Now get out." I obey her command and leave her to sulk on her own.

Chapter 14: Amethyst

Date: March 31st, 2024

When I awake, I am relieved to find that I am feeling better. I've been feeling moody and ill for the past day, and the wait until we can go to the mines is killing me. Not literally, but now that I'm healthy and happy again, I am rearing to go and explore.

I shower, change, and brush my teeth eagerly. I don't even dilly-dally in the pristine hotel room, with its white-on-white design.

Feeling refreshed, I yell down the stairs, and race after my voice. "Max!" I search for him in the breakfast area, where he is half-heartedly poking at his eggs and bacon. It's not the hand I damaged. I join him when I have a plate full of pastries, toasts, and a bowl of cereal. "Good morning." I smile, once again forgetting that he can't see me. My belly rumbles- I barely ate anything yesterday.

"F-finally." He sighs. "A-after a whole day you finally c-come and eat without c-complaining."

"I see ya also feel wonderful." I roll my eyes.

"J-just bored." He sighs and slowly eats his remaining eggs. I shovel down my food with hunger. Max, on the other hand, is slow as a snail on the back of a turtle trying to win a race against a sloth.

"Come. We can get ya some stuff whilst we're out."

"O-ok." He nods slowly.

"What's up with you?"

"N-nothing." He seems to snap out of his chain of thoughts. "I-I was t-thinking about how I'll manage t-to g-get back after all t-this is over."

"You'll figure it out." I assure him, not really caring whether he even survives after we part. I drag him upstairs. "Grab the plans, and list of items we need."

"W-we have both memorized everything we need, t-though." He cocks his head to one side but picks the items up from the bed-side table without a lot of fuss.

"Better to be safe than sorry."

"I-It would be safer to not take them." He stuffs the notes into my bag.

"How?"

"D-do you want someone to find these plans?"

"Exactly why I want to take them with us." He slumps onto the bed. "Are ya definitely ok?"

"N-no." He finally admits. "I-It's Easter Sunday."

"It is?" What's so special about this Sunday? "Umm, could ya explain what that means?"

He blinks twice in disbelief. "E-excuse me?"

"What's Easter?" I ask again. I have only been in this time since late September, how am I supposed to know?

"T-the holy week Jesus was c-crucified and resurrected?" He asks, as if to jog my memory in some way.

"The guy who was born Christmas day and whatnot?"

"E-exactly!"

"What do you mean by 'who was crucified'?"

"I-I'll explain later. B-but basically, everyone c-celebrates t-that he c-came back from t-the dead on Easter Sunday."

"How did he do that?"

"H-he's t-the son of G-god." He tells me, as if that explained everything.

"Do you pray or something?"

"N-not really. S-some people go to church. B-but my family always had- has, an Easter egg hunt. G-gemma is always t-the best at it, and t-then we eat c-chocolate." He smiles sadly, as if his whole family is dead, and not only his poor granny.

"That sounds surprisingly fun." What should I say to him now? This sounds like a very emotional topic, that could end in tears. "Do you want me to hide some scrambled eggs from breakfast around the room?" Max laughs softly, making my heart melt. I wish I had a freezer to put it in.

"N-no. B-but t-thanks for t-the offer." He stands up again. "L-let's g-go hunt some elements!" That must be an upgrade from *eggs*.

"Hoorah?" I say uncertainly.

"Y-yeah, I don't know." We awkwardly shuffle out of the room, and out of the hotel.

I hail a taxi like in a movie, and we climb into the musty-smelling car. "D-do you want to know about Easter?"

"Sure." I give the address to the driver who coughs loudly and unnaturally at the prospect of driving to the mines.

"Cosa farai nelle miniere?" I give her a blank stare. "English?"

"Yes, please."

"What will you be doing at the mines?" I am able to understand her English perfectly, though she has a strong accent.

"Visiting them." I tell her.

"Sorry, but you're going to have a problem. They're closed off to the public."

"We're not going inside." I lie. The driver shakes her head, clearly perplexed by why you would go to caves if not to go inside. She starts up the engine and I tell Max to continue talking about 'Easter.'

"A-a long, long t-time ago..."

"Here you go." The driver tells us after two hours of driving.

"Thank ya." I pay her the fee.

"T-thanks," Max adds. We head towards the caves, and I feel the urge to yell and shout at the top of my lungs into the empty area. For miles, there are no buildings and only two or three people around.

There is plenty of greenery, fresh and bright, but the ground is rocky and dry, creating an interesting contrast. The mouth of the caves peer out of the ground, leaving only a small entrance, which has yellow tape wrapping around it. The tape has the words 'DANGER. NO ENTRANCE.' written all over them.

"No one's watching." I tell Max.

"T-there are people here?" He sounds stressed.

"It's fine," I whisper. "They aren't paying us any attention and I'm pretty sure they're even less innocent than us."

"W-what are t-they doing?"

"I'm not quite sure, but it looks like they're hiding something here." I grab Max's arm, which makes my heart flutter, and I duck under the tape, letting Max bump into it. "Come on!" The feeling is thrilling, breaking the rules. It's pitch-black inside, and I can't even see my feet. I feel as blind as Max.

"Good day." A soft and delicate voice says from the darkness, in a way I would imagine a flower to talk. "I really am sorry about this."

"W-who is t-there?" Max stammers.

"I also can't see. It's too dark." My feet lose touch with the ground, and my breath quickens.

"I really am sorry." The voice repeats.

"Who are ya?" I scream, thrashing in the air. "Let us go!"

"I'm sorry, Morana."

"Ya got the wrong person!" I kick and flip in the air. "Let us down!"

"I can't do that, Morana."

"I'm not Morana! Who on Earth is that?"

"Earth might be the wrong word, Morana."

"Stop calling me that!" My mouth suddenly flies open, and a silent scream slips out of me as my body shivers involuntarily. I feel my legs, arms, and torso squeeze as if I were attempting to slip through a solid wall. I can't feel Max in my grip anymore, and I can't get my hand to move. My stomach flips and my head spins.

Finally, it's over, and I fall onto the floor.

Chapter 15: Amethyst

Date: Unknown

"Stay here." Someone says and I see a young girl who looks wrong and messed up. She is blurred around the edges, and she has the wrong number of arms; She has six. SIX ARMS! She is closer to resembling an insect than a human. Even weirder than that, she has no mouth, ears or nose. How did she even speak to me? And hear me? Why doesn't she have legs? Is that a fog, instead of legs? Is she a genie? No, she can't be. I don't think genies are bald. It's hard to tell that she's a girl with her haircut and style. Only her voice lets me know.

"Who-" Get your words together, Amethyst. "Who are ya?"

"Do you not remember me?" She looks disappointed, but I've never seen her in my life. I shake my head. "I'm Uki." I try to figure out how she's talking without a mouth when I realize that I can't feel the ground. It looks shiny and smooth, but it feels like I'm lying on air.

"Where am I? Where did ya take me?" I attempt to stand but collapse from the effort. "What?" I am not weak. What happened to me? Why won't my legs move?

"You don't remember." It is not a statement, nor a question.

"No..." I think she would have given a sad smile if she had a mouth. She twists one of her six hands at a weird angle, as if trying to get it through the bars of a cage and leaves it hanging in mid-air. What does she want me to do with her hand? Shake it? Pull it off? I would be happy to do that. If I had any strength left in me.

"There is a cage there." She informs me. "You simply don't experience it in your dimension."

"What?" She takes her hand away, her eyes turning from silvery gold to metallic blue. "How did you do that?" She shrugs and drifts away. "Come back!" I yell. I have too many unanswered questions. "Come back!"

"Don't worry. You won't be alone for long." She disappears through a surface I can't see, her gold dress disappearing last. This must be a dream. What dimensions? What cage? How is a bug-human talking to me without a dumb mouth?! I stretch my hand out, but there is nothing there. She must be kidding me. I want to run away or wake up, but I don't even have the strength to breathe. Why am I not breathing? Am I going to die? Am I dying? Am I dead? I close my eyes and make myself breathe, even though it pains my lungs, like someone is pulling them out.

"My dear Morana." A terrifying voice calls from not far away. That name. Again. Who is Morana? "We have so much to talk about." The voice is like pins stabbing into my brain it's so chilling and evil.

"Can we start with introductions?" I open my eyes to see pure black ones looking back at me. Into me. They belong to a man who looks as distorted as Uki but clothed in black from head to toe. Only his pale face is exposed. I notice that his fingers are long and spindly, as he holds onto something I can't see (the invisible cage).

I think he would have grinned if he had a mouth. A malicious, blood-curdling grin. "You're very *pretty* in that body." I shiver from the cold he lets off- it's like an ice statue.

"I asked for introductions."

"I am sure you remember me." He puts emphasis on the sure.

"I assure ya not." I also stress the 'sure'. His eyes flicker from wicked to heartbroken in a split-second then they turn back.

"My name is Horace." He lets go of the cage and reaches his hand into it as Uki had done, but instead of leaving it hanging, he winds his stick-like fingers in my braids. "We both know your name, luckily."

"I don't think so. I'm not Morana."

"So tell me, not Morana, what are you called down there on Earth?" Down there? Where are we? Are we up? Up where?

"My name is Amethyst, ya idiot." He tugs gently at my hair, as if he had never touched a braid in his life. "And I want to go back."

"I'm so sorry, dear." Why did he call me dear? "But you can't. And neither can your little friend." The word 'friend' seems to make him want to vomit.

"Where is Max?" I ask. How is this the first time I'm thinking about him since I got here? "Is he ok?"

He uses his other hand to, what looks like, unlock the cage.

"For now." Horace, as he calls himself, pulls my head towards him by my braids, and I hit his chest. Pain floods my head as my braids are almost pulled out, yet I don't feel him when I crash. I still can't feel him even when he starts to stroke me. "I've finally got you."

"Let. Go. Of. Me." The words come out in gasps. Does he want to kiss me or kill me? Who is he?

"No." He replies simply. "I won't let you leave again." He tugs my chin upwards, and he's too close to my face for my comfort.

"I don't know ya. I never left ya. But I don't blame Morana for doing so." I attempt to kick him, but my legs fail me. He chuckles. "Tell me. Who is she?" I demand. I'll wait for him to loosen his grip. I have nothing else to do.

"*You* are a Celestial." Morana is. Not me. "You are as powerful as me, here."

"I'm not!"

"So sorry for the misunderstanding." My whole body freezes as his strokes go lower, going from my cheek to my neck and chest. "I thought you would remember." He thinks for a minute and I stay quiet. Silence is power.

As if he were done playing with me, he throws me back into the spot where I layed a minute ago, and mimes shutting a door.

"Uki!" He yells, this time his voice sounding different. More frightening, less creepy. "Take her to the Meadow Veil. Hopefully she'll remember who she is there." Meadow Veil sounds too nice to be a torture device, but what else could it be?

Uki drifts back into the room, a tiny horse-like creature now sitting on her head. "Yes. Of course." She peers at me with her big eyes, which are now an identical colour to mine, and then she is calling me to come as if I were a kitten.

"Good." Horace decides. "I'll see you soon." He floats away.

"I'm sorry." She bursts out as soon as he's gone, like 'sorry' will take back kidnapping me and preventing me from saving humanity. "I had to." I still stay silent. "Let's go." I stay still. "He can hurt you. You have to do what he says." She plays with the animal which had flown down to one of her hands. It resembles a butterfly and a horse simultaneously. "You may not remember, but he has hurt you before, and he'll do it again."

"It's not me! I'm just Amethyst! Not Morana!" She grabs my hand, which I can only see, but not feel, and drags me with surprising strength for such a petite girl. I feel like a young child, being taken home after an outburst in public. I try to escape the Uki's grip, but we're stuck together like glue. I want to cry. I want to scream. I want to thrash around. I want to run. But I can only be dragged along the floor, through walls, and across pavement.

"Let me go!" Uki looks at me pitifully and lets me get captured by Horace once again. The beautiful garden does not improve the situation.

Chapter 16: Max

Date: unknown

I am stuck.

I can't move.

My limbs don't listen to me.

I can't feel anything.

I can't do anything.

I am helpless, like a child stuck in the middle of a war. Only a young girl comes to talk to me, but all she says are a few timid words, but I know instantly that she is the one who brought us here. I don't know what I'm supposed to do: I am lying in a silent darkness, unable to do anything but think. I think about where Amethyst is, whether she's ok, and whether she can move. I am sure that if she could, then she would beat the girl up.

Honestly, a year ago, I wouldn't have believed the mess I've gotten myself into, and what real problems are in the world. Getting less Easter chocolate than your sisters is nothing compared to this.

A squawk penetrates the silence, shattering it into a thousand pieces. What was that? Where did it come from? Has it been hours? Minutes? Days? That's how long I haven't heard, seen or felt anything. I thought I had gone deaf, too, for a while. Something squawks again, but closer to me. Fear churns in my gut.

"Max." A disembodied voice enters my ears, but instead of making me feel better, I get even more terrified. "Max." It's horrible and makes me want to curl up in a ball and cry.

"Y-yes." My own voice is croaky in my throat from not talking for ages. "H-how do you know my name?"

"I've been waiting for you for a while. I hope you've had a warm welcome." Yet another squawk, then the sound of a trumpet. "You're blind?" He sounds shocked, my unfocused eyes giving my disability away. Does this give him an advantage?

Who is there? Stay away! Is what I want to tell him. "Y-yes." Is what I actually say.

"I didn't give you all the credit you deserve, then."

"F-for what?" I rack my brain for anything good I've done in my life.

"You know, Time Machine? Does that ring a bell?" He chuckles menacingly.

"I-It does."

"Good. Now that's all confirmed, I would like to say goodbye for the first and last time."

"W-what?"

"You have to go." He sighs. "You have made a big problem for me, by making your little toy."

"W-who are you?" I whisper, petrified, my heart thump-ing.

"Horace." The room suddenly feels empty, and I think he is no longer here. A series of squawks sound from nearby, and my heart does somersaults and flips as I realize this is the end. Not only for me but for all of humanity. And there is no one to save me this time. I'm going to get beaten up by a bird, and there will be no one to save me, and nobody will get the girls back to the beginning of humanity.

Was it all hopeless from the start?

I don't keep my tears back, and I let myself wish I had stayed with my mum. I would stay alive. I would be happy. I could find a way to be happy on my own in a world where there is no one. But either way, it ends like this: no more people to walk the face of the Earth.

I squeeze my eyes shut and wait for the impact. But it never comes. No pecks from a bird. No limbs are being ripped off. The squawks have even stopped, but I don't relax. I am still in flight or fight mode, despite being unable to fight or fly.

"Get up." A sing-song voice calls, contrasting the mood of fear.

"I-I c-can't."

"Sure, you can. Just let your brain forget that you 'can't move'. The only thing stopping you is your mind." Why is she singing?

"Huh?" That's the worst piece of advice ever.

"Convince yourself that you can move, and that you just have to try."

"H-how does t-that logic work?"

"I learned that from *your* kind. Also, who cares about logic? Do you want to stay here, or go?" Good point. I have nothing to lose, so I will myself to get up and walk. "Be careful." She adds quickly, but as I stand, she gives a high pitched "Okie." Like there was something trapping me, but it didn't work on me.

"W-what?"

"Never mind. Follow me."

"U-um. I-I c-can't."

"We just discussed that you can." She's still singing, though in anger. Could she be cursed to sing? No, that's impossible.

"I-I don't know where t-to g-go."

"Follow me!"

"I-I'm blind, woman!"

"Ah. It would have been much simpler for you to just say it, than, you know, not say it." Fingers wrap around my wrist, but it feels different to Amethyst's hold. It's gentle, and I can barely feel it, as if a ghost were holding me, and not a woman. Even though it feels different, I have to remind myself constantly that it's not Amethyst. She is not here.

We run.

"W-where are we g-going?" I ask after a good ten minutes of jogging, completely unaware of where we're going.

"Far away from here."

"W-why are you helping me?"

"It's what Morana asked Uki for. I overheard. And also, because there is a group here supporting you and the girls." I can almost tell that she has a sparkly smile on her face, even though I am narrowly escaping death. If she isn't a trap. Then I'm jogging towards my end.

"W-who is t-this Morana girl? A-and other girls?"

"Your friend. The one with the braids." She ignore my other question completely as we turn a corner and start to slow down.

"T-that's Amethyst."

"No. That's Morana."

"A-amethyst. H-how would you know?"

"She's a gifted Celestial, like us. And our friend."

"W-who? W-what are you?"

"My name is Valda."

"A-and what is a Celestial?"

"I can't really tell you that. You'll find out one day, but not right now." I'm always in the dark on everything! As an afterthought, she adds, "We're here."

"W-where?"

"Uki."

"I-is Uki a person or place?"

"Celestial."

"W-what does t-that mean? A-are you not human?"

"It's difficult to explain."

"Valda. Stop with the chit-chat. We need to get him out of here." It's the shy girl who came to visit me earlier. She doesn't sound so timid now.

"W-what about Amethyst?"

"Who?" Uki asks, as if it were as confusing for her as it is for me.

"Morana. That's her human name." As if that explains anything.

"Oh." Uki exclaims. "She's fine, for now. As long as she listens to Horace, she'll be fine."

"T-the Horace who wanted t-to k-kill me?"

"Wants to kill you," Valda confirms.

"T-that definitely makes me feel better."

"He really is the detective, isn't he?" Uki says. Was that sarcasm or not? "No wonder Horace hates him. Though I was expecting him to be more like a dashing prince charming, like in human stories."

"Same." Valda agrees, and lets go of me, leaving my ego bruised from their comments about me, though I don't even know them.

"W-what will happen t-to Amethyst if she doesn't listen t-to Horace?"

"Don't worry about that just yet. She won't die, if that's what you're wondering. Why do humans always worry about death?" Valda sings and chuckles, leaving my side.

"I-Is t-that supposed t-to make me feel better?"

"Never mind that. Just let me get him back home..."

"B-but I need Amethyst!" I interrupt Uki.

"She can't come with you." She tells me. "Her place is here."

"N-no, it's not. S-she is a major part of the plan! W-without her..." I can't do it.

"She has more important things to deal with here. Like keeping Horace at bay." Valda insists.

"I-If she doesn't come back with me, all of humanity will die." Silence. Something seems to pass between the girls.

"We know that." Uki soothes, "How about we make a deal? If she gets put in danger, we'll send her to you."

"S-sure." I am in no position to negotiate. And I don't doubt Horace will put her in danger soon enough. There is another silence, where Valda and Uki seem to have a whole conversation without even using their words.

"Ok." Valda seems to come to a final decision. "She will go to Earth, but later. Max." She addresses me. "Have you seen the others down there?"

What others? I think, then I remember the other girls that were in my memory. "N-no," I admit. "O-only when I t-travelled t-to t-the past..."

"Where are they then? Did something bad happen to them?" Uki starts to panic.

"Calm down, Uki. They're tough. Tougher than us. We agreed on that."

"I know, but I haven't seen them in Celestia at all. Not during their time, and not ever." This sounds like a riddle, where I am missing the question and half the clues.

"We'll get Max back, for him to work on his... thing, and then we'll get Morana to join him when she's ready." I am relieved to know that I'll see Amethyst, (Morana? Whatever.) again, but can I trust these people/not people? They could be with Horace for all I know.

Too late. I'm spinning again, and my head is close to exploding. Some sickness almost comes up and I feel the squeezing sensation again.

I roll onto the ground, completely clueless about where I am. How am I supposed to even find my way around without Amethyst to guide me? I brush myself down and realise I don't know what to do. Until I hear shuffling.

"H-hello?"

"Are you ok, kiddo?"

"I-I t-think so, but I c-can't see anything. I-I'm blind, you see, and I need some help."

"Ok. Then how did you get here?"

"W-where am I?"

"A hotel room. I'm cleaning it right now."

"W-what hotel and number is it?"

"Silicad. Room 124."

"Ah. T-this is mine t-then." I feel around and find the man's hand and pat it. "T-thank you. C-could I be left alone now?" Stunned, he leaves me to my thoughts.

I've basically gone backwards in the plan, but at least the girls kept the first half of their promise. I feel so useless as I feel my pockets and find my phone. At least I have my phone. Even if I don't have dignity, sight, Amethyst or much money.

Chapter 17: Amethyst

Date: Unknown

That was the most incredible thing I have ever experienced. I love the Meadow Veil. Who knew being a prisoner of an evil man could feel so good? Being here is not so bad now that I can move, and that Horace isn't grabbing onto me constantly. I could stay here, easily. I don't really care about being the first human anymore, it's too much responsibility. Here, I am practically free. At least, I am free from Max's yapping, and that must count for something.

I walk through fields of purple clouds in which little fairy-like buildings peek through them. Golden rays of divine light illuminate paths of shining crystal (which lead to mystical gardens and Meadow Veils). As I see Horace, my heart flutters and I push through the small crowd of Celestials to get to him.

"Would you like to go to the Meadow Veil today?" Horace asks me. He's honestly not as scary as I thought he was: he let the Mr Whine-o-saurus Max go. I wouldn't have. I would have killed him, personally, after all he did.

"I can't say no." I laugh, grabbing Horace's arm. It doesn't make me shiver anymore, but grin "You wanted to meet up?" I ask in my sweetest voice.

"Oh, yes. Thank you for reminding me. It's about time I got you to work."

"Work?" I stop walking. I thought I was free here. Of course. How could I be this stupid?

Like always, Horace seems to read my mind, "Don't worry, dear. It's not the kind of work humans do."

"Oh. Then what will you make me do?" I joke.

"Let's say, you'll help me cut the string." I wonder what that could mean.

"Sounds better than house chores." I roll my eyes and catch up to him with a renewed bounce in my step. Horace looks into my eyes, and he weaves his fingers between mine.

"It is so rewarding." He says and I wish Horace could smile. It would make my day, every day, though I can't be truly sure when the days start and end since time is so confusing here.

I only manage to keep up with what the date is using Uki, as Horace won't let me know. Goodness, she is so annoying. Sometimes, she is and yappy like Max, but then others, she is the most loyal servant you will ever meet. She isn't my servant, not yet, but on occasion, she can act like one, if I give her a little shout. Today is supposedly the 16th of January 0010A.D and the 4th of April 2024, plus some others. Here, for some reason, there are multiple dates at once, but what do I care? I've left Earth behind for good.

"I'll see you later, ok?" I inform Horace.

"Yes. I'll see you at the Meadow Veil when Uki calls you." He winks, sending shivers down my spine (but not in a bad way).

"Bye." I let go of him, but my arms want to reach out to him and hold him tight. "Uki." I snap my fingers and she is there. "I would like to see the Queen today. I have a request for her." I stride towards the place I've been staying at in my spare time recently, and Uki rushes to keep at the same pace as me.

"I wouldn't recommend today. She is in... a pirate phase." She trips over a cloud that sticks out like a sore thumb, but unfortunately, she doesn't fall flat on her face.

"What? I have never heard anything so ridiculous!"

"What do you want from the Queen, anyway?"

"It's none of *your* business." I snap. What I want isto be free. Free of responsibility. I don't want to have a job, or have to do something for someone else because I have to. I want to be able to do what I want to, when I want to. Horace is great, but I want to be independent and feel like a member of this society, not a prisoner. Whatever he says, I don't want to work; I've had my share of damn hard work.

"When can I see her, then?"

"Whenever, Morana. I mean Amethyst." She adds quickly. "But I would recommend giving her a few days."

"No. I'm going today. Tell her I'll be there in a little while." I have a meeting today that I have to attend, but I really don't want to go. I'm only going because Horace asked me to.

"I'm not your messenger." She backs away from me.

"Then find someone with the power of communication!" I yell at her. "It's not that hard."

"Yes. Of course." She drifts away and I head towards the meeting area that I have grown accustomed to during my time here: it's where I eat, meet and relax. It's large (larger than my house on Earth) and very empty most of the time.

"Zosia." I greet her with fake excitement.

"Someone's in a good mood."

"I'm not. I just need your wisdom." I say truthfully and drop the act.

"Of course. That's the only thing anyone wants me for now-a-days." She sighs.

"Tell me, who can predict the future here?"

Her eyes widen. "What do you want?"

"Why do ya need to know?"

She tuts, and happily says, "There isn't anyone like that. Not even Horace knows what's in the future because humans are too unpredictable." Dumb humans! Why is she so glad about that? "Anyway, we don't need to know. Only *humans* have that kind of want." She better not be calling me a pesky human.

"How about a creature, then?" I spit in her face. I am not ready to give up.

"Nope."

"Ya must know. You're wisdom!" The room starts to fill with Celestials.

"I don't. I know everything that is to know. Not what will be to know. And you better believe me: I can only tell the truth."

"That makes zero sense."

"Sit down!" Yells Riki from the front. "Or I'll kick you out!" I roll my eyes. He wouldn't, and though I don't care about the threat, I take a seat to get away from Zosia.

⧖

I head in the direction of the grand castle that I can easily see above all the clouds and buildings. The towers are painted gold and brown, which is a new feature. Probably like that due to the Queen's 'Pirate phase' as Uki had said. The castle is so tall, that I can see it from almost everywhere in Celestia. It doesn't matter if it's the beast sanctuary, Horace's Parqui, or even the Library of History.

I wonder about what my power was before I became a pathetic human. Horace told me I was incredibly important, but some other Celestials brainwashed me into becoming a person. One of the first people, to be precise. Now that I think about it,

Max is probably my very distant descendant, and the thought makes me sick. How could anyone with my blood be so ridiculous and pathetic?

I march through the pearly white gates and don't even stop to admire the scenery and piratey oddities like murals of captains and costumes. I swing the throne room doors open, avoiding the gaze of the guards who look at me with curious expressions. Not everyone is used to, or accepting of, a human girl being up here.

"Your Majesty. I must talk to ya." I look at her. She looks as if she were a nine-year-old girl in a pirate costume from Amazon. I shake my head and dismiss how funny she looks. I open my mouth to speak, but the Queen beats me to it.

"Morana! Me 'earty."

"Excuse me?" How did she recognise me? Horace informed me that I look drastically differently from my Celestial form.

"My friend!" She comes down from the throne which looks fit for a mermaid and hugs me.

"Hello?" My arms stick out awkwardly between her three sets of them. "I, um." I am startled by her claim of us being friends, but I take it as an opportunity. "Hello. I have a request." Do I bow? Do

I curtsy? Who cares? She's my friend apparently, so it doesn't matter.

"Yes?" She looks at me eagerly.

"I would like to have some sort of pass so that I don't have to do work." I say simply, and she starts to laugh.

"I may not be the person to help you with that."

"How come? You're the Queen! Ya can do anything!"

"Not quite. I have to be a Queen and a ruler, not only for a country, like humans, but every person that has ever existed. I have responsibility, and so do you, and so does everyone that exists. We can't stop having it."

"But," I stop myself. But what? Now I feel supid, flustered and embarrassed.

"What would you like me to do?" She asks kindly, which hits a nerve.

"I don't know." I admit bitterly.

"Are you sure? Maybe you would like to get a house, or a parqui, or your own..."

"No."

"But you must have had a plan when you came here." She turns around, flipping her golden hair and starts to climb the stairs that are painted bright blue to match an ocean.

"Turns out my plans always fail." I mutter, turning and leaving.

I sit right outside the Furgiana room (which is next to the room I left a little while ago), leaning against the wall. I think it's meant to be impossible for Celestials' minding to access the information inside, but my human ears can hear the noise inside almost perfectly. It's all mushed together, but I catch a few words here and there such as 'Pet', 'Health' or 'Luck' and I figure that this is the room where 'Prayers' are 'Answered'. I even manage to decipher a whole wish, 'Please let me do well on my exam.' and I presume Zosia answers, when someone says, 'I grant him wisdom.' How weird it now seems that exams are the worst thing in somebody's life.

This whole place makes me consider whether Max's God exists, or whether it's the Celestials who take on that role. I curl up into a ball, tucking my legs under my arms. I've been wearing the same clothes ever since I arrived here, since everybody wears either a dress with six arm holes or a top and no leggings. I don't how much longer I can go before having to resort to make-shift outfits. Celestials are odd, but I feel like I've started to adapt to be like them in some ways: I've stopped breathing and going to the bathroom, because oxygen and nutrients are not needed here. I'm starting to miss water, though, and my mouth is always dry.

I'm swallowing my own saliva when a tall, handsome Celestial addresses me like a dirty beast. "Human!" He comes out of the room next to Furgiana: the room where they decide the future of the world. And Zosia said that no one knows the future. "How did you get here?"

"I'm with Horace." I sigh, barely lifting my head from my knees. That's what I have been instructed to say whenever someone asks me why I'm here.

"Sure, sure. Get lost. Humans are not allowed to know the future."

"I know that. But I don't care about the future. I'm from the past." I roll my eyes.

"Morana?" I nod, finally lifting my head to look him in the eye. "You always use the purple eyes! Welcome back!" He takes my hand and shakes it, leaving my little ball of comfort broken. He winks, suddenly in a more open mindset about talking to me. I roll my eyes again and leave. "Hey! When are you going to come back to help me?"

"I don't know." I reply truthfully, not even knowing who he is.

"Do you remember me, Fortune?" I shake my head as I exit the building.

I head to the Centre Parqui: the one where the first Celestial who floated to the edge of Celestia started his journey. Apparently, he's been drifting across Celestia for seventy-eight hundred thousand years. But there's no 'edge of the Earth' so why would there be an 'edge of Celestia'? This dude is probably going to make some stupid story up; he has had enough centa-milleniums to think of a realistic yet exciting one.

I try and avoid the growing crowd, as I don't want to have to explain what humans are and why one is here to someone who hasn't even realised the world has moved on.

I pass past the Parqui with almost no attention being drawn to me, and I manage to catch a fraction of a rumour that 'There are other Celestials, very far away. But they are wild." But I don't hear much else because most conversations are minded or in another language. Some Celestials used their logic and learnt a few languages to drive away the boredom of living for eternity.

Soon, I arrive by the sea-like place I like to call Heaven. A girl from school (whose name I can't remember) once told me how she imagined it looked like, and this place almost matches the description. Lilac clouds a shade lighter than the rest in Celestia tackle one another playfully, and together they look like waves crashing into each other. The sky is as blue as a sapphire, and there are pearl-like stars hanging just above the little cabin bobbing in the middle of the cloud-sea. I sit down and let my hands dangle just above the clouds as I look for the girl who sews hearts with ruby thread. I often can glimpse her from here, but right now, she must be out on a ruby thread shopping trip.

I watch the fake sun and moon chase each other across the sky, bumping into the stars on occasion. Even an emerald little dragon-like creature comes to sit on my lap and lick my hand. With my still-dry hand, I stroke its furry scales, carefully avoiding its spiky tail. All too quickly, Loba finds me and informs me that Horace wants me to come 'cut the string'. I couldn't care less about anything right now, but I follow him reluctantly.

"What do I have to do?" I snap at Horace, still in a bad mood from my failed trip to the Queen today. It gets even worse in the darkness of Horace's damp cave where he works. I don't feel like doing a job, and I have a strange feeling that I have been wrong about something for a long time. Watches hang from the ceiling, dangling as they shine a bright gold.

"Just cut right here."

"Why?" I cross my arms across my chest protectively. Why does it say Max's full name?

"Well, because it's your job. Don't you like it? You control so much, and yet do something so simple."

"It sounds very boring." I think I sound like a kid, but I don't care.

"You're the only one who can do it."

"Making me feel special is not going to make me do it."

"It's your power."

"You're lying." I look at the delicate golden watches. They all have names written on them, and they are all at different heights. "These strings and watches have no meaning."

"Are you sure?"

"Stop messing with me!" What if Horace sets the watches' times, and I... end the person they represent?

I think about Queen Gina, how happy she was despite having to be the most responsible in all of the dimensions. I think about how Horace is so careless with his title and power as Time Master. I want to be like Gina, responsible yet happy, but I don't know where I will be content. Here, with Horace, or on Earth, with Max. What do I love more? Do I even know what Love is anymore? Have I ever known? Will I ever know? I feel like curling up into a little ball again but this time crying and yelling. Why can I never get the one thing I want? Freedom from responsibility. Wherever I look, all I am is a tool, and I have a job to do.

Should I help humans, or end them?

I look at my cut from when I destroyed the flowers. But they were flowers. What would happen to me if I killed humans?

All I truly know is that I want to see Max. I don't care whether that comes with the biggest amount of responsibility ever and a bunch of his yapping.

"Sorry. I have to go." I try and excuse myself.

"You can't." Horace turns even colder than the first time I met him. I want to punch his ugly face, but I restrain myself. "I need you." From his sleeve he pulls out a shining object, and my heart and stomach mix around in my body. "I need you." He repeats but more slowly. The knife is now in full view, but I can't move, and I'm rooted to the spot. "Stay with me forever." I start to back away slowly. "It won't hurt." He whispers menacingly, and steps towards me faster than I can back away.

"Stay away." I whimper as he grabs onto me by the waist. Why did I think he was great? What came over me? I would fight him if I could get my hands out of his grip.

"Stay still." Chills crawl up my spine (this time in a bad way) as I try to wriggle free of the slowly approaching knife. In a panic, I bite Horace's arm as hard as I can, unsure what else I should do. He screeches as the knife slips out of his grip, but I stay firmly in place. I lean forwards, then back, and elbow him where his cheek would be.

I fall to the ground.

Head and heart pounding, I run. Horace attempts to throw the knife, but I dodge it with ease, knowing perfectly well that he must have little-to-no experience with weapons. Unfortunately, I'm the same.

He catches up, but I palm-heel strike below his chin, and he topples back like a domino brick.

I side-step through the wall, careful to not break eye-contact until we can no longer see each other. I am glad that the door in Horace's dimension will slow him down if he chases after me. I run through gardens and roads. I run until my legs can't carry me any further. I run until I am almost spotted by the Celestial who crossed Celestia. I run until I collapse onto a bench, heaving giant breaths, though it doesn't do any use here. I lay down, my hands behind my head, and my feet dangling off.

Luckily, three familiar Celestials come into view, and I almost cry in relief. I am not planning on dying today. I just need to hope that Uki, Zosia and Valda are on my side, not Horace's.

"Good day." Valda sings with a smile, "Nice for you to pop round." I give her my best death stare and turn to Uki.

"You're ok, now. I'll send you to Earth right now. Max is waiting."

"Max?" I gasp. That must mean he's alive. "He's ok?"

"Yes, dear." Zosia pats my shoulder comfortingly, "But he needs you to help him. And soon."

"You know about what we're doing?" I ask in disbelief, though I know that Zosia knows 'everything that is.'

"Why do you think Horace wants to kill you both so badly?" Valda laughs heartily.

"Let's get you to Earth." Uki tells me. I put my finger in the air to indicate for her to wait. I don't want to go back to a life of responsibility and pressure, now that I know what I'm missing out on up here. I have freedom here, except for Horace. Before I can come to a final decision, Uki snaps her fingers on all six pairs of her hands, and the last thing I see before I'm gone are the three girls, looking at me with sisterly care, even when I've been horrible to them.

I'm flying back to Earth to yet another round in this helpless fight.

"Thank you." I manage to whisper before I'm in the hotel room again.

Chapter 18: Amethyst

Date: April 4th, 2024

When I arrive, Max is in the bathroom, so I decide to take a seat on the bed and wait. My head is still swirling, and I hear Max's voice drift from the bathroom, singing. I smirk as he starts to sing a verse of Wrecking Ball, the false notes hitting my eardrums like hammers. I join in as the chorus starts, and we sing "I came in like a Wrecking Ball!" Together for about a minute before Max stops abruptly.

"W-who's t-there?" He asks quickly, finally realising he isn't in a Disney Movie, where back-up singers appear out of nowhere. "A-amethyst?"

"That's me." I call.

"Y-you were singing."

"So were you." Silence. There's shuffling in the bathroom, and the door clicks open.

"I-I need a t-towel." He says shyly "I-I left it on my bed. I-I wasn't expecting you t-to appear out of nowhere whilst I'm in t-the shower..."

"No hello?" I laugh and throw the towel over my shoulder, heading for the bathroom door. I try not to imagine Max without clothes on as I give the towel to his arm which peaks out from behind the door. He snatches the towel from me and locks the door behind him. I try not to blush.

I wait for him on my bed, swinging my legs around, taking in the smell of Earth. I let my stomach rumble, ready to have food after days in a food-free zone.

$$\text{⧗}$$

Chapter 19: Max

Date: April 4th, 2024

I change quickly, barely drying myself after being startled by Amethyst's sudden appearance. I feel flustered after she had to pass me my towel. "What took you so long?" She asks me when I come out fully dressed, and very wet. I must look a mess. My hair hasn't been combed in the days she was gone, and I have only eaten breakfast- no lunch or dinner.

I want to ask her the same: she has had me waiting for her to return for three days, probably having the time of her life up in the clouds. "I-I..."

"I was just kidding. Good to see ya again."

"G-good? I-I t-thought you hated me."

"Well, like an annoying piece of fungus, you've grown on me."

I smile, "I-I missed you t-too." She hugs me for a strangely long time; her arms hold me tight, as if she didn't want to let go, and the ends of her braids tickles my face. After a long while, I pat her back, and she –reluctantly? - lets go of me.

"Let's go get that Sanium, and get out of here." She playfully punches my shoulder, a non-verbal, non-visual gesture that it's good to be back. It's so simple yet says so much about how our relationship has improved.

Date: April 5th, 2024

We spend the few hours before dark watching some news and playing along with some game shows. (I did better than Amethyst, even without being able to see. She gets offended when I bring it up. How embarrassing for her). But, when the clock hits nine, we drop 'dead' like mice (not really). We sleep so hard; someone wouldn't believe it if I said that it's not an official step in our plan. For all we know, we may not get another slither of sleep until we're in Anceint Egypt. If all goes well, we'll be in Ancient Egypt.

We calculate that our money will perfectly last us four taxi rides and a lunch. "We planned this perfectly!" Amethyst exclaims as we finish doing the math, stuffing our mouths with breakfast. Why should we not fill ourselves with free all-inclusive food when we've done a good job? We've survived going to the place some would call 'Heaven' or 'The Land of The Dead'. Only a few more hours, and our Time Machine should be done.

"Y-you're right." I grin.

I hope that Amethyst wears the same smile as we sit in the taxi, nervous and excited simultaneously.

We're so close to doing the impossible.

Chapter 20: Amethyst

Date: April 5th, 2024

"No one's watching." I tell Max.

"T-there are people here?" He jokes. It feels like we are recording a movie, and we are taking the scene again.

I grab Max's arm, which reminds me of last time. I duck under the tape, letting Max bump into it. "Come on!"

It's dark, but this time we brought flashlights with us. I switch mine on, and the cave's cracks and crevices are revealed. We walk steadily onwards, and the back of my mind feels as though we should come across Uki again.

The light catches on something, and it shimmers mesmerizingly. Sanium. In all its purple-scarlet glory.

I pull on my gloves as I inform Max. "We have found the Sanium. Proceed with caution." A bright light other than my phone's torch burns brightly so much that I have to shield my eyes. "Max!" I yell. "Ya damn stupid idiot! I told ya to proceed with damn caution!" I run up to him and grab his arm. It's terribly singed and half is hand is *gone*. "Damn idiot. Just stay still and I'll collect the Sanium quickly. Then we'll go back to the hotel."

I make sure my glove is on, then I grab the Sanium with quick precision, and slide it into the graphene container. "Done. Now let us get ya bandaged up."

I look to the roof of the cave warily and see distinct shapes of rocks. Rocks that seem to loosen more as I stare at them. One falls from its place.

I push Max towards the exit, careful not to not burn him again. I quicken the pace when rocks start to fall behind us, at first a couple, then many, like a waterfall of stones. I pull him out of the mouth of the cave and slide myself behind him just in time. I barely avoid trapping my leg.

Chapter 21: Amethyst

Date: April 5th, 2024

"Ts." I hiss as Amethyst bandages my throbbing hand. I'm glad that I'm blind for once, because I can easily imagine what it must look like: raw muscle and flesh peeking out from beneath a layer of skin that is no longer there.

"Sorry." She pats my hand painfully when it's fully covered in bandages. "That should do for now."

"W-why must I always g-get t-the injuries?" I pout. "I-I am always on t-the wrong side of t-the world's anger."

"Serves ya right for touching Sanium."

"I-I c-couldn't see where it was!" I moan.

"Stop being a baby. You'll survive." I huff as she says it. "Don't complain. Now I get to do everything else without ya, ya realise that?"

"I-I never was much help, even when I c-could see." I mumble under my breathe.

"I'm going to find out where we can find a forge." Amethyst stands up, switching to her own bed, and I hear the clicking of her unlocking her phone. "There's one a half hour drive from here, and the brute looks like he wouldn't care if teenagers used it."

"I-If you say so." The 500g of Sanium in the Graphene pot feels like it's not enough to save the world. The excitement and nerves in my gut feel strong enough to destroy the universe if they were let outside of my body. I can't believe this is happening.

⧗

Making the case takes much longer than I expect, but we get there in the end. Melting, forging, polishing, filing, measuring, the list goes on and on about the tedious task we complete. But it's now done: we have a time machine in our possession. My heart is thundering inside my chest like a stampede of elephants.

"Do you think it'll work this time?" Amethyst whispers when we're out in the open- this forge is placed so weirdly that it only takes a minute for us to be away from civilisation.

"I-I hope so." I squeak back. "A-and why are we whispering?" Why would anyone be listening in on a pair of teenagers in the middle of nowhere?

"I have no clue. It feels right." She laughs "This *thing* is so crazy and mysterious and deserves respectful silence." She turns serious.

"W-what does t-that mean?" I don't remember it looking that incredible.

"I don't know." She locks her fingers in my uninjured ones, sending my heart racing even faster; I don't think it can cope with all these emotions, and it may fly away at any moment.

"Are ya ready?" I nod stiffly, hardly able to speak, feeling my sweaty palm against Amethyst's.

"R-remember. W-we're g-going t-to Ancient Egypt. L-look out for hieroglyphs." She squeezes my hand to remind me that she knows that.

"Where's the on button?"

"I-it's t-the natural dent t-that is made in t-the side."

"Ah. Now I remember." Click. The plants and the ground itself pull us down, as gravity strengthens for just a moment. I brace myself, and the pressure is suddenly gone. The feeling is like travelling to and from Celestia.

⧗

Suddenly, we're sitting in a wooden compartment- the cart, I later realise- and we're slowly moving along tacky train tracks. They're probably prehistoric.

"W-we, did it?" I ask, already knowing the answer.

"We did it." Amethyst sighs in awe, "And it's unbelievable."

Acknowledgements:

I cannot describe what I'm feeling right now: this is my first book and I'm over the moon! It has been in the works for what feels like both an eternity and just a few days, and my whole heart has been put into this. This plot has been through so many twists and turns that I can't believe it's finally a professional piece of work. There are so many people I could thank, but here is just a few who are, honestly, the most incredible people I think I'll ever know.

Firstly, I would like to say thank you to my bestest friend, Sarah. You are literally the best individual I could be friends with, as you read this book first and gave me amazing feedback. Honestly, I don't know how I managed to live without knowing you, because you are the nicest person ever and words are not enough to say how thankful I am for you. I don't know who my beta reader would be they weren't you. Thank you. (See? I mentioned you!)

Secondly, Ali, my not-so-little sister, for being surprisingly supportive about this whole journey. I love you so much. And even though you don't listen to my blabbing, I'm thankful for you as you sometimes don't tell me to stop. Also, I'm grateful for your help with spelling and grammar in this book, and I hope your dreams will come true, especially since you helped mine. Thirdly, my mum. Thank you for EVERYTHING. You supported me, gave life to me, and trusted me to do this. And you also made food for me every day as I wrote, and I'm glad that you tell me before you start making it because I always take forever to get downstairs. I love you so much, and always remember that, even if/when I hit a crazy teenager phase. Next, I would like to say thank you to my dad because you pay for all the equipment I use and if I ever need something, you're the one I talk to. I'll be surprised if you ever see this message, because you never read books, but maybe you'll read this one for me? Pretty please? It would mean the world to me. Lastly, anyone who reads this and enjoys it, because when I was writing, I kept thinking of you. I kept writing for you, so that someone who

wants to read a book like this will have it.
Thank you so much for your support.

www.ingramcontent.com/pod-product-compliance
Lightning Source LLC
Chambersburg PA
CBHW020656120726
47906CB00001B/297